Three days since we last came here, Haruhiro thought.
"This wasn't here," he said. "Not last time."
Haruhiro turned his lantern towards what should have been a rock
wall. The light was sucked into the darkness and vanished. It
looked pretty deep.

"Uh, well," Shihoru started hesitantly. "Haruhiro-kun, congrat...ulations?"

"No, it's not..." Haruhiro stopped. His mind went blank, he couldn't find the words.

"Hooooh," Yume's eyes went wide. "Yume doesn't really get it, but it feels like somethin' to be celebratin.'"

"Congratulations," Merry said, in a deadpan tone for some reason.

"Grats," Kuzaku said, suddenly bowing his head.

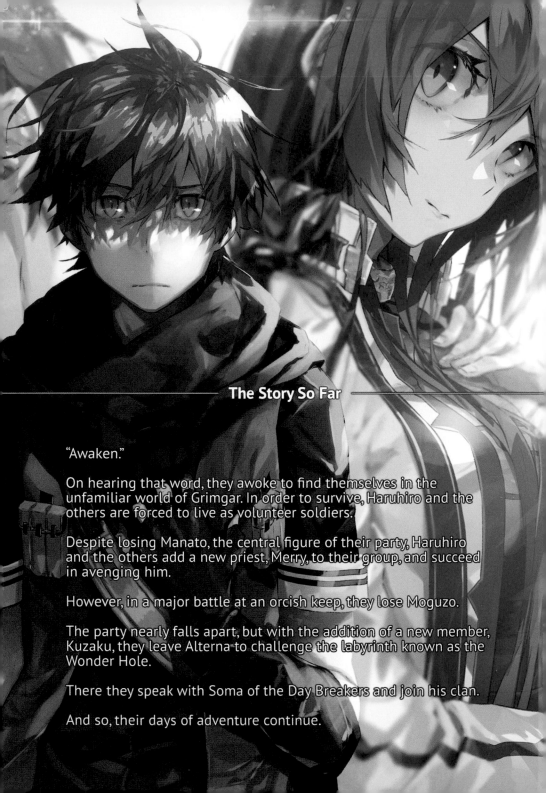

The Story So Far

"Awaken."

On hearing that word, they awoke to find themselves in the unfamiliar world of Grimgar. In order to survive, Haruhiro and the others are forced to live as volunteer soldiers.

Despite losing Manato, the central figure of their party, Haruhiro and the others add a new priest, Merry, to their group, and succeed in avenging him.

However, in a major battle at an orcish keep, they lose Moguzo.

The party nearly falls apart, but with the addition of a new member, Kuzaku, they leave Alterna to challenge the labyrinth known as the Wonder Hole.

There they speak with Soma of the Day Breakers and join his clan.

And so, their days of adventure continue.

Grimgar of Fantasy and Ash

level. 5 — Hear Me Out, and Try Not to Laugh

Presented by
AO JYUMONJI

Illustrated by
EIRI SHIRAI

GRIMGAR OF FANTASY AND ASH, LEVEL. 5

© 2015 Ao Jyumonji
Illustrations by Eiri Shirai

First published in Japan in 2015 by
OVERLAP Inc., Ltd., Tokyo.
English translation rights arranged with
OVERLAP Inc., Ltd., Tokyo.

Seven Seas books may be purchased in bulk for promotional,
educational, or business use. Please contact your local
bookseller or the Macmillan Corporate and Premium Sales
Department at 1-800-221-7945, extension 5442, or by
e-mail at MacmillanSpecialMarkets@macmillan.com.

Follow Seven Seas Entertainment online at gomanga.com.
Experience J-Novel Club books online at j-novel.club.

Translation: Sean McCann
J-Novel Editor: Emily Sorensen
Book Layout: Karis Page
Cover Design: Nicky Lim
Copy Editor: Tom Speelman, J.P. Sullivan
Proofreader: Maggie Cooper
Light Novel Editor: Jenn Grunigen
Production Assistant: CK Russell
Production Manager: Lissa Pattillo
Editor-in-Chief: Adam Arnold
Publisher: Jason DeAngelis

ISBN: 978-1-626926-83-7
Printed in Canada
First Printing: January 2018
10 9 8 7 6 5 4 3 2 1

[TABLE OF CONTENTS]

Characters

YUME

Airheaded soothing-type. Speaks an iffy sort of Kansai dialect?

Class: Hunter

HARUHIRO

Sleepy eyes. Passive-type. Provisional leader.

Class: Thief

SHIHORU

Shy and withdrawn. Hard worker with little presence.

Class: Mage

RANTA

Selfish, flaky joker. #1 most unpopular.

Class: Dread Knight

MERRY

Cool beauty. Has more experience as a volunteer soldier and is a little more of an adult.

Class: Priest

KUZAKU

The new guy. Hard to tell if he's motivated or not.

Class: Paladin

Other Characters

Team Renji

Renji — Class: Warrior
Head of Team Renji. Wild beast-type. Dangerous.

Ron — Class: Paladin
The Team's No. 2.

Sassa — Class: Thief
Flashy woman. Probably an M.

Adachi — Class: Mage
Wears glasses.

Chibi — Class: Priest
Mascot.

Team Tokimune (Tokkis)

Tokimune — Class: Paladin
Handsome. Friendly optimist.

Inui — Class: Hunter
Looks middle aged. Has middle school syndrome, maybe?

Tada — Class: Priest
Fighting priest. Real showoff. Kind of a serious headcase.

Mimori — Class: Mage
Ex-warrior mage. Nickname is "Giantess."

Anna-san — Class: Priest
Blonde-haired, blue-eyed, self-proclaimed pretty girl.

Kikkawa — Class: Warrior
Good at getting by in the world. Enlisted at the same time as Haruhiro and the others.

MOGUZO

Bear-type.
A somewhat slow,
but reliable bear.

MANATO

Kept the party together.
Was a good guy.
(Past tense)

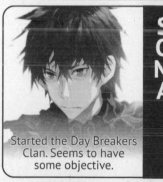

SOMA

Started the Day Breakers
Clan. Seems to have
some objective.

CHOCO

Did Haruhiro know her?
Fell at the orcish keep.

Grimgar of Fantasy and Ash

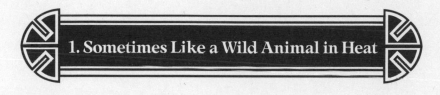

1. Sometimes Like a Wild Animal in Heat

The enemy was—black.

No, not black; blackish, and he wore something that looked like a raincoat.

He stood maybe 2.5 meters. Pretty tall.

More or less, you could've called him humanoid.

He had a head that was oddly small, as well as arms and legs. His shoulders were awfully broad. His body shape couldn't have been more of an inverse triangle.

He was holding a weapon with a long handle. The blade was like a thick, sturdy knife, and, well, it was basically a naginata. He was leaning over, using his naginata like a cane as he walked.

There was no sound to his steps, and even as his naginata dragged along the ground, it made no noise. For some reason, he was silent. It was a mystery why, but Haruhiro had just decided to accept that was the way it was.

"Well, shall we?" Haruhiro asked.

Kuzaku let out a deep breath, lowering the visor of his close helm.

Whew...

From deep inside Ranta's skull helm—its visor had a skull-like design, so as a servant of Lord Skullhell, that was what Ranta had decided to name it—there was a low, menacing laugh. He'd become fond of laughing like that, recently. Maybe he thought it made him sound cool. Maybe he was an idiot. Yeah, probably the latter. He'd always been an idiot, and he probably always would be.

Yume drew an arrow from her quiver, nocking it to her elven composite bow. She was still better with her machete than her bow, but she'd purchased a new bow along with her new machete a little while back. She'd learned two archery skills, too. Even if she wasn't the best suited for it, she seemed to be trying to do something about that.

Merry checked the glowing mark on her left wrist that indicated her Protection spell was active, then made the sign of the hexagram. "O Light, may Lumiaris's divine protection be upon you...Assist."

Instantly, another little hexagram of a different color appeared on Kuzaku's left wrist.

The enemy must have heard Merry's chanting. He was coming their way, picking up speed as he approached.

Shihoru began to chant and draw elemental sigils with her elfwood staff. "Ohm, rel, ect, delm, brem, darsh."

A hazy black elemental erupted forth, and it enveloped Shihoru's body thinly. Armor Shadow. It would only work once, and there were limits to what it could handle, but it could neutralize an attack. For a lightly armored mage, it was a defensive spell that could make a world of difference.

The enemy was already getting close. Soon, he'd be in striking range with his naginata.

"Get out there, Kuzaku," Ranta said.

Rather than respond to Ranta's spurring him on, Kuzaku moved forward with big, relaxed strides.

The enemy swung his naginata. Kuzaku didn't back away. He stopped, and held out his shield. He didn't so much block the naginata as knock it aside with his shield. It wasn't the Block skill, it was Bash.

There was an incredible clashing sound, and the enemy's naginata was knocked flying.

Kuzaku thrust out his sword towards the enemy's exposed torso. The enemy leapt back with hardly a sound.

Yume let loose an arrow. It struck him in the left shoulder.

Haruhiro headed to the enemy's right side, while Ranta tried to advance on his left. The enemy didn't like that and withdrew even further.

"Now!" Merry cried. Of course, everyone knew what she meant.

"Suuuuuuuuuuuuuuuuu…"

The enemy emitted that bizarre sound. Both of his arms stretched. During that interval while they were stretching, he was wide open.

"Press in!" Haruhiro called.

Haruhiro circled around behind the enemy. Kuzaku put his shield up in front of himself and charged. Ranta was—

What, again? He sure likes doing that.

"Bwah heh heh heh…! Slice…!"

He swung a longsword—which Ranta had decided to name Betrayer, just because its hilt was blackish and the name kind of suited it, even though the sword was only of decent quality otherwise —as if he were drawing a figure-eight, a sword skill that was certainly showy.

If it were any dread knight other than Ranta using it, it might've even looked beautiful. Ranta's vulgarity lowered the grace and dignity of the Slice skill. But that was fine, as long as he wasn't dragging down its power as well.

Betrayer sliced up the enemy's right arm. Kuzaku's longsword gouged the enemy's flank, as well. The enemy's left arm and head were tough, but the rest of him not so much; a blade would go through.

By the time the enemy's arms had extended to half again their original length, Haruhiro had taken up position behind him. He wouldn't attack immediately. It wasn't time yet.

While Haruhiro was lying low, Kuzaku and Ranta moved in closer and closer. When the enemy was in long-arms mode, infighting was the best strategy.

Yume fired off another arrow, hitting him in the right shoulder.

Is he coming? Haruhiro thought.

About two seconds later, the enemy tried to pull back, but Haruhiro was right there in the direction he was trying to retreat. It seemed he had forgotten that Haruhiro even existed.

Haruhiro had been using Sneaking to try and get the enemy to forget, or to not notice him. It had paid off. Haruhiro was able to cling to the enemy's back, stabbing his dagger into the enemy while he was still processing what had just happened. Haruhiro gave the dagger a sharp twist and he tore it free, then stabbed it back in again.

The enemy was probably going to do a vertical jump to try to throw Haruhiro off. He bent his knees and lowered his hips. That was a sign it was coming.

Haruhiro leapt clear before the enemy jumped.

The enemy sprung into the air for a half-hearted jump, then

immediately lowered his posture again.

"Suuuuuuuuuuuuuuuuuuuu…"

Both arms shrunk. That was another opening.

"Punishment!" Kuzaku shouted.

"Hatred!" Ranta bellowed.

Kuzaku and Ranta both sprang at the enemy at practically the same time, swinging their swords down diagonally. Kuzaku's longsword struck the enemy hard on the head, blowing away his hood, while Ranta's Betrayer dug into his right shoulder. After that, they both got in another two or three hits, then pulled back when the enemy's arms finished shrinking. The metallic skull that was his head was now clearly visible.

"Jess, yeen, sark, fram, dart!"

It was Shihoru's Falz Magic. Lightning. The enemy was struck by the bolt and twitched.

His mouth opened, but his teeth were clenched tight.

Chik, chik, chik, chik, chik, chik, chik, chik, chik, chik, chik, chik, chik, chik, chik, chik, chik.

He started clicking his tongue.

"Kuzaku!" Haruhiro called.

Kuzaku replied, "Yup," and charged at the enemy.

The enemy was in the middle of raising his left knee. That was the motion he made when preparing for a jumping knee kick. When Kuzaku crashed into him with his shield, the enemy was knocked over.

"Nicely done!" Ranta yelled with a vulgar laugh as he attacked the enemy.

Kuzaku was using his longsword to whale on the enemy, too.

Haruhiro made a decision. *Let's finish him here.* He wasn't really

trying to set a record for time or anything, but it seemed pretty doable, and even if the enemy fought back a little, the party could more than recover from it.

Was he being overconfident? No. This was an enemy they had fought several times now. They more or less knew what made this one different from the others by now, well aware of how little variance there was between the different members of its race.

The ustrels.

He wasn't getting carried away, and after the first time they'd met this kind of monster, Haruhiro never would've imagined a time would come when he might think this.

They're no match for us now, he thought confidently.

"We're ending this!" he shouted.

When Haruhiro made that declaration, Yume drew her machete and closed in. Merry readied her short staff, not leaving Shihoru's side.

The ustrel, of course, was trying to get back on his feet, but every time he did, Ranta would jeer and kick his arms or legs out from under him, keeping him from getting up.

Ranta always does these things with such glee, thought Haruhiro. *It must come from his nasty personality.*

Kuzaku was focusing his onslaught on the ustrel's head and neck, not so much slashing him as bludgeoning him. Kuzaku had always been blessed with a tall, strong body. When Kuzaku swung down his longsword with all his might, the destructive force behind it was considerable. He lost the ability to talk when he got focused, but that wasn't a shortcoming. Kuzaku silently continued grinding down what life force remained in the ustrel.

"Meow! Raging Tiger!" Yume called.

This skill of Yume's, where she did a somersault followed by a powerful blow on the enemy, was pretty dangerous. Every time he saw it, Haruhiro thought, *It's amazing she's not scared to do that.*

While keeping an eye on his comrades, Haruhiro occasionally stared at the ustrel's back. This was, well, just a habit. No matter what they were up against, if he observed closely, he could figure out what kind of creature it was—or at least he felt that way. It was only that he felt that way, and it couldn't possibly be true, but it was strangely calming to stare at his enemy's back.

Once in a while, a strategy would come to mind as he did it. Like, *This guy seems weak here,* or, *He has this idiosyncrasy in the way he moves,* or, *This is where we ought to attack him.*

And then, rarely, he would see that line. To be more precise, it was a dim light that was something like a line. It seemed to be a visualization, of sorts. *My opponent will move like so, and has this sort of a weakness, so I should do this.* It was a sort of instantaneous prediction. One he processed as if it were a single line.

Setting aside the question of whether it was actually a line or not, apparently, everyone had these sorts of visualizations. Generally, they were easier to see when in a difficult situation. In some cases, he'd heard, it was possible to see multiple lines. In other words, some people could instantaneously make multiple predictions.

It differed from person to person. By a lot, actually.

Regardless, it was an ability every thief had. Nothing special.

Of course it wouldn't be, Haruhiro thought. *I'm fine with that, really.* Haruhiro wasn't disappointed at all. *A special ability that only I have. It would be nice to have one, of course, but I doubt I'm going to have one. And, as a matter of fact, I don't. That's all there is to it. I don't have what I don't have.*

That said, if you were to say I—we—have nothing, that wouldn't be true at all. We might come up short in the quantity, quality, and variety of what we have when compared with a genius, but even ordinary people don't have nothing. They have to make do with what they have. There are things ordinary people can do. Ordinary people can grow. We can get stronger in our plain, ordinary way.

There was a harsh, screeching sound. The ustrel was already foaming at the mouth and chattering his teeth. He was on the verge of death.

"Take that, and that, and that, and that, and that!" Ranta yelled.

He vigorously stabbed Betrayer into the ustrel's back over and over. Kuzaku backed away, looking to Haruhiro. Haruhiro nodded. There was no need to waste more energy than they needed to. The ustrel was dying. Ranta could handle the rest. Ranta loved thoroughly tormenting a dying enemy and then snuffing the life out of them.

It wasn't like Haruhiro didn't question if he should really be acting like that, as a person, but his cruel mercilessness had helped them occasionally. Of course, if you asked Haruhiro whether he liked the guy or not, the answer would be that he truly hated him with every fiber of his being.

"Oh yeahhhhhh!" Ranta shouted, mounting the motionless ustrel and starting to do something. Probably trying to get his hands on some loot.

That said, ustrels were not a good source of money. The only things they had that were worth a good price were their metallic skulls and the naginatas they carried. Both of those were bulky, and not worth the trouble of hauling back. Especially the metallic skulls.

They might look like helmets, but they were actually something like an exoskeleton, and they couldn't be taken off, so you had to carry them back with the head still inside. They'd tried it just once, but for all the effort involved, they'd been disappointed with the minimal return on it. Haruhiro never wanted to do that again.

What Ranta wanted was to take a piece of the ustrel's body, just because keeping trophies was his disgusting fetish—no, not really. Dread knights took an ear, claw, or other small piece of the enemies they personally killed to give as an offering to Skullhell. They accumulated vice that way, which let them learn dread knight magic and fighting skills, or strengthened their dread knight magic with Skullhell's blessing.

Well, he's a brute, Haruhiro thought.

In a group of twenty volunteer soldiers, you'd be lucky to find even one dread knight. It was easy to see why there were so few of them.

I couldn't stand doing that, Haruhiro thought. *Unless it really suits your personality, you can't go on as a dread knight.*

Worse still, even if you couldn't go on, anyone who became a dread knight could no longer change to another job. They were forced to swear their loyalty to Skullhell alone, and to never betray him so long as they lived. In other words, their code said they couldn't stop being a dread knight. If he left the guild, his fellow dread knights would chase him down. He'd be killed.

Scary. Dread knights were too damn scary.

"Eh heh heh heh heh!" Ranta cackled, lifting up something coated in blackish blood. A tooth from the ustrel, apparently. Haruhiro covered his mouth with the back of his hand, fighting the urge to vomit.

Yeah, I'm sure he'll be just fine, Haruhiro thought. *The job really suits him. Actually, he's a dread knight to the core. It's his calling, I'm sure of it.*

With Ranta's work done, Haruhiro and the party decided to leave the ustrel's remains and move on. This was the edge of the muryan nest. The muryans would clean up the body, no doubt.

The Wonder Hole. It'd been more than four months ago that they'd first set foot here.

Honestly, it wasn't very profitable. Actually, they were using all their earnings on food, drink, baths, equipment, and occasional trips back to Alterna to learn new skills.

The Lonesome Field Outpost had a branch of the Yorozu Deposit Company and, if they were willing to ignore the high fees, they could withdraw the money they had on deposit at the main branch, but their savings hadn't grown at all. Worse than that, Haruhiro's had gone down, and he wouldn't be surprised if his party members' had, too.

We can go in a bit deeper now, Haruhiro thought. *Kuzaku's gotten used to the party, and he's now a functional tank. Each of us have gotten stronger in our own way, to the point that we can easily wipe the floor with an ustrel. We're making steady progress... Maybe?*

It's hard to say. I think we're going at a good pace, though. Sometimes things don't go well, and that can be a real mess. There are times when I agonize over what to do, too. Then there are also times when I just accept that thinking too much isn't going to change anything, and focus on that day's work.

Are things okay like this? he wondered. *The answer to that question changes every once in a while. Right now, yeah, it's fine, or at least not bad, I'd say.*

Not bad. At least, it shouldn't be.

Haruhiro was standing at the front of the group, keeping a watchful eye on the area around them as they progressed through the muryan nest with its many side tunnels. Because that ustrel had appeared, the muryans had all retreated. They wouldn't show themselves.

"Man…" Ranta said, with a sniff of his nose. "Things have gotten, I dunno, kinda repetitive, haven't they? Lately, that is."

"…Here he goes again," Shihoru said with a sigh.

"Huh? Did you say something, saggy tits?" Ranta asked.

"Th…they are not saggy!" Shihoru exclaimed.

"I dunno," Ranta said. "I haven't seen them. You'd have to let me check 'em out for myself. Yeah, that's it. That's what you've gotta do. Can't say for sure that they aren't saggy otherwise. Am I right, Kuzacky?"

"Could you stop it?" Kuzaku asked. "Don't call me that."

"Kuzackyyyy!"

"What are you, a little kid?" Kuzaku asked.

"I. Am. An. Adult. I'm an adult, no matter how you cut it. I'm so adult, I'm *way* too adult. You can tell that, right, Kuzacky?"

"Man…" Haruhiro said, cursing himself for butting in when he knew it'd do no good. It was best to just stay quiet. Of course, he cursed Ranta even more than that. Half a billion times more. "Can't you do anything other than bother people? Aren't you ashamed to live like that, as a person?"

"I'm not ashamed, clearly," Ranta said. "I do it with pride, and you know it. I live without showing restraint towards anyone. Can't you tell that, you moron?"

"You're a fine example of evil thriving," Merry said coldly.

"Your hate," Ranta said with a deep, sinister chuckle, "it gives me strength. Do you get it? That's because I'm a knight of darkness, a dread knight. I am the darkness. Got it? By the way, Yume, Shihoru's tits—they're saggy, right?"

"Huh?" Yume furrowed her brow, and then, probably without thinking, brought her hands to her chest and made a gesture like she was lifting something heavy. "Wait, there's no way Yume's gonna tell *you* that, Ranta, you perv!"

Haruhiro hastily looked away. His eyes met with Kuzaku's by chance. They had an unspoken conversation.

"...Just now, they looked pretty heavy..."

"Yeah. Really heavy..."

No, no, no, no, no, Haruhiro thought insistently. *Stop. It's awkward thinking about that sort of stuff with my comrades. It's better if I don't think about it. I shouldn't think about it. If I think of them as men and women, it really does get awkward. But, well, with Kuzaku—*

Haruhiro glanced over to Merry. *Hmm. I wonder. I don't really have any decisive evidence one way or the other. Not that I've tried to find any. I mean, they're free to do what they want, yeah? That's why, though I don't know what's going on for sure, Kuzaku leaves the tent at night sometimes. When I quietly follow him, sometimes he and Merry are talking outside. Just the two of them. I've spotted them doing that a number of times.*

I dunno, but it feels like they're making surprisingly little progress...? Though, that said, it's not like they aren't both conscious of each other in that way.

Of course, they're free to do that stuff. Haruhiro told himself that they should do whatever they wanted. He had only tailed Kuzaku those first few times because he'd been concerned for the man, as a later addition to the party. Like, that he might be feeling out of place.

I mean, wouldn't anyone worry in a situation like that? Haruhiro thought. *I'm supposed to be the leader and all. So, from that, it seemed like Merry was giving him advice, and I thought, "Oh, good." But, is it just advice she's giving him?! Is that really all?! If they've got something going on, I wish they'd tell me! I wish they'd stop sneaking around behind my back! I mean, I'm curious... I do feel that way somewhat, but, well, I guess it's fine?*

It is fine—isn't it?

Like, you know, it's fine while they're getting along and all, yeah? But, if they break up or something, won't that be awkward? Or maybe they'll be able to compartmentalize?

Will they? Haruhiro didn't know. *I don't have the experience. No, I don't remember life before coming to Grimgar, but I probably don't? That's what it feels like. I definitely didn't have a ton of experience. That much I can say for sure. There's no way a guy like me was popular with the ladies. I mean, I'm not now. Sometimes, I get the feeling that Yume, Shihoru, and Merry don't even see me as a member of the opposite sex. And what's wrong with that?*

It was actually more convenient that way. It meant that when something happened in the party, Haruhiro was the only one who could approach the girls with the same emotional distance that he did the guys. If things got bad between some of the others, Haruhiro could stand in the middle and try to mend fences.

It's a pain in the butt, and I do wonder why I should have to, but I'm the leader, he told himself. *I have to accept it. I'm well aware that I lack what you'd call leadership skills. But a good comrade, a relatively good friend, someone who values the harmony of the party, and who, even if he can't pull everyone along with him, finds a way for us all to struggle forward together, that sort of central figure... that's what I aspire to be.*

Well, I think that's what I'd like to be, if I can. Only if I can.

"Saggy tits," Ranta sang. "Saggy, saggy tits. Saggy. Tits. Saggy. Tits."

If I didn't have stupid, stupid Ranta, and his weird, crappy song, it probably wouldn't be that hard, you know? I'm gonna Backstab you, pal, Haruhiro thought viciously. *No, ignore him, just ignore him. That's always for the best. Everyone's figured that out by now. Even Shihoru's holding it in. Sorry, Shihoru, that you have to put up with that piece of trash. They aren't even sagging. They don't sag, right? Though, if they're that big, you can't fight gravity forever...*

No, no, no, stop. Haruhiro shook his head.

The stone walls ahead were neatly carved out to look like buildings. No, not *like;* they were buildings. Quite impressive ones, at that. They'd almost reached the kingdom of the devils.

"Ranta, we're passing straight through, got it?" Haruhiro asked.

"...Yeah, I know already," Ranta said. "You don't have to tell me every single time. I just messed up a little bit that first time."

And because of it, we ended up in real trouble, thought Haruhiro.

Haruhiro and the others set foot in the kingdom of the devils, which resembled a temple carved into the side of a cave. From the windows of the buildings, someone—many someones—were looking their way.

Not humans, of course. While they were built similarly to humans, their legs and nether regions were covered with thick fur, and they had goat-like horns on their heads. They all had staves that they carried with them everywhere. They were called staves, but some were like bludgeoning instruments, while others had spear or sword-like blades on the end. They were all quite imposing.

Baphomets. Also known as devils.

"Hello, hello," Ranta said with a forced smile, and then, the exact same voice came back.

"Hello, hello," a devil said.

Ranta hadn't repeated himself. It was the work of a devil. They didn't necessarily understand human language, but they were amazing at imitating voices.

"Hey, stop that!" Yume cried, jabbing Ranta in the back.

Another devil spoke in Yume's voice. "Hey, stop that!" it said.

The devils weren't especially friendly towards humans, but they weren't hostile, either. However, whenever a human said something, they would imitate them like this. It wasn't clear why. They might have thought it was amusing, it might've been a natural trait of theirs, or perhaps they were looking to see how people would react. Honestly, it was a bit irritating.

All the devils would do was watch humans, thoroughly imitating their every utterance. Before they'd reached this kingdom of devils, Haruhiro and the party had acquired that information. Frustrating though it might be, so long as the party didn't start anything themselves, having their voices imitated would be the worst they'd have to deal with. In that case, all they had to do was shut their mouths. If they were silent, the devils would be, too.

Of course, that had been the plan. The devils had a great love for architecture and sculpting, and they valued their staves highly. However, aside from their staves and stone crafts, they had little of monetary value. There were a lot of them, too. Killing them would be pointless.

Despite that, after being imitated just a few times, Ranta had snapped and started shouting.

The devils must have interpreted it as a hostile action, because they had come and attacked. Haruhiro and the others had managed to escape somehow, but ever since then, whenever they approached the kingdom of the devils, the devils would gather around to intimidate them. In fact, they had been attacked twice and forced to retreat. Haruhiro had thought they were going to die one of those times.

They went through the valley known as the domain of the three demi-humans to reach the muryan nest, but without passing through the kingdom of the devils, they couldn't go any further. The kingdom of the devils had a complex layout. No matter how capable a party was, it would be difficult to get through it if they had to fight devils all the time. That was why they maintained good relations with the devils. Everyone did, and Haruhiro had meant to do the same, but because Ranta acted like a total moron, the devils hated them now. Worse yet, the devils seemed to have good memories, and they weren't about to forget what Haruhiro and his group had done. Even if Haruhiro and the others tried to wait for that enmity to die down, there was no telling how long that might take. They had tried everything to get the devils in a better mood.

"Ugh, these guys piss me off... Can we just kill 'em?" Ranta muttered in an oddly cheery tone.

"Ugh, these guys piss me off... Can we just kill 'em?" the devils imitated.

"He's a certified idiot," Shihoru said darkly.

"He's a certified idiot," the devils imitated.

"Seriously, man, cut it out..." Haruhiro said with a sigh.

"Seriously, man, cut it out..." the devils said, even replicating his sigh perfectly.

"But, seriously, this has got to piss you off," Ranta cackled. "Ha ha ha!"

"But, seriously, this has got to piss you off. Ha ha ha!"

"You can just plug your ears," Merry said, her tone colder than ice.

"You can just plug your ears," the devils imitated, no less cold.

"How about you try not talkin' in the first place?" Yume said.

"How about you try not talkin' in the first place?"

"Shut up, Tiny Tits."

"Shut up, Tiny Tits."

"Don't call them tiny!"

"Don't call them tiny!"

"This is going to drive me crazy..." Kuzaku muttered.

"This is going to drive me crazy..."

"If this is enough to drive you crazy, you sure are weak, Kuzacky! You beanpole!" Ranta hollered.

"If this is enough to drive you crazy, you sure are weak, Kuzacky! You beanpole!"

"Please, would you just shut up?" Haruhiro said, plugging his ears so he wouldn't have to hear the devils imitating him. It didn't help.

"Please, would you just shut up?"

I can still hear them pretty well, you know, Haruhiro thought. *Is there something special about the devils' voices? I don't know why, but putting my hands over my ears barely blocks them. I'm not Kuzaku, but I really do feel like this is driving me crazy. Actually, if Ranta would just keep his mouth shut, nobody else would say anything. This is Ranta's fault. Everything is always Ranta's fault.*

Haruhiro struggled to maintain his sanity as they walked through the kingdom of the devils. There were lights shining out of the windows, so it was fairly bright, but the roads were narrow and twisted, making it hard to see ahead. Sometimes what he thought was a road wasn't a road, too. There were a lot of dead ends. If he let his guard down, they'd get lost in no time. He had considered trying to make a map, but he had to give up on the idea. He didn't have a good grasp of distances or direction, so it would be too hard to draw a map. It would probably be impossible, short of measuring everything out.

A low-end estimate for how long it took to pass through the kingdom of devils was 40 to 45 minutes.

I think we've been walking forty-five minutes already, Haruhiro thought.

The cave's temple-like buildings had ended a little ways back, and it had grown darker. Haruhiro pulled out a lantern to light their way.

"Huh...?" he said.

That's weird. Haruhiro stopped. He shined his light around the area.

"This is the mineshaft, isn't it?" he asked. "It should be..."

"How should *I* know?" Ranta spat out. "You're the one leading the way, Parupiro. We're following you because we trust you. If you're saying you've betrayed our trust and taken us to some weird place you don't know, tthen that's a big problem, pal—a big one. It's your responsibility! Now ritually disembowel yourself to apologize, you moron!"

"We took the right path...or we should have," Shihoru ignored

Ranta and agreed with Haruhiro. "If I'm not wrong, at least..."

She didn't sound all that confident.

"Hmm." Kuzaku turned around. "I don't think you're wrong. Personally, that is..."

He did not sound very confident either.

"Wait, hold on." Yume looked around restlessly. "This isn't the mineshaft? Wasn't the mineshaft like this?"

As for Yume, it seemed she didn't even remember what the mineshaft she had already visited several times looked like...

"There's something different about it..." Merry said, cocking her head to the side. "...Maybe?"

She didn't sound confident at all.

"It's wrong," Haruhiro said, sure about that now.

The mineshaft.

It was called the Grimble Mineshaft, to be precise.

The name came from creatures called grimbles that lived in this area. They were like huge rats, but with rock-hard skin and shells on their backs. Some rare individuals had gold, silver, and diamond in their shells, which of course sold for a high price. However, because of excessive hunting, their numbers had dwindled—or that was the common belief, but it seemed that their population was showing a recovering trend recently.

That was what Haruhiro and the others thought, anyway. This was their seventh trip to this mineshaft. The past six times, they hadn't seen any diamond grimbles, but they had spotted a gold grimble once, and a silver grimble on four separate occasions. They clearly weren't on the verge of extinction. While the group hadn't managed to catch any yet, even the silver shells were worth a lot of money, so what was the harm in trying?

However, whether they were gold or silver shells, it would be best if, once they succeeded in catching one and gained the necessary know-how, they managed to gather as many as they could and sell them all at once. If it looked like there was money to be made, a number of other parties would probably rush to the mineshaft. If that happened, Haruhiro and his party probably wouldn't be able to compete. They needed to make a tidy profit before then.

That was their plan. And they'd come to the mineshaft to catch gold or silver grimbles.

That was how it was supposed to be, Haruhiro thought. *It's been three days, though.*

They couldn't afford to spend multiple days in a row doing nothing but search for grimbles. If they went too long without fighting a difficult battle, their combat senses would start to dull.

Three days since we came here, Haruhiro thought.

"This wasn't here," he said. "Not last time."

Haruhiro turned his lantern towards what should've been a rock wall. The light was sucked into the darkness and vanished. It looked pretty deep.

"...This hole," Haruhiro said.

"Like! I! Said!" Ranta shouted emphatically. "You got it wrong! Boroborwo! You took the wrong path! This isn't the mineshaft, man! I mean, they call it a mineshaft, but it's just an ordinary maze-like cave-like thing! They're all over the place! This place just looks similar! That's all it is! Use some common sense!"

"No, but..."

I didn't take the wrong path—I don't think, Haruhiro thought. *I'm confident... But, well, why is this hole here when it shouldn't be?*

It was three meters across, and more than two meters high. There was no way they could have overlooked it. If they'd passed by it, they would've been guaranteed to notice. It was a big, round hole.

Haruhiro looked left and right. Like Ranta said, the mineshaft was like a natural cave, with nothing special about it. It had no special characteristics that made it stand out, nothing that he could use to recognize it at a glance. So, though he couldn't say anything definitive, aside from the existence of this hole, it was no different from before, he thought.

"Someone," Yume said absently. "They came and dug it, don't you think? This hole."

"Like they could!" Ranta kicked the ground. "Who'd dig a hole! Here in the Wonder Hole! Like anyone has the time! Think a little before you talk!"

"You say that, but the Wonder Hole's just a big hole, too!" Yume shot back.

"Hm...?" Ranta crossed his arms and cocked his head to the side. "Now that you mention it, I guess so...?"

"It might not have been a human," Shihoru said in a conspiratorial tone. "There could be all sorts of creatures here digging..."

"Wow," Kuzaku said, poking his head into the hole. "Sure is dark. Y'think there's something in there?"

"Hold on." Merry pulled on Kuzaku's arm. "That's dangerous."

Yeah, just show off how close you two are, Haruhiro thought.. Or, that's something I may or may not have thought. No, I'm not thinking it, okay? It's just really awkward. Though, it's something I could warn you not to do, you know? Uh...maybe?

But, when Haruhiro cleared his throat a little, Merry seemed to snap to her senses, turned around, and let go of Kuzaku's arm.

Huh? Huh, huh, huh? Haruhiro thought. *Why is she awkwardly trying to put some distance between herself and Kuzaku, I wonder? Maybe it really is awkward for her? Did I get in their way? Maybe I should say sorry? Not that that's what I was trying to do.*

Haruhiro sighed.

I should stop, he thought. *I mean, it's almost like I'm jealous. Not that I am. I mean, yeah, I was interested in Merry. There was a time when I felt that way. But, well, she's clearly out of my league, you know? Though, if I had to say whether I like or hate her, I'd say I do like her. Like, if Merry asked me to go out with her, obviously, I'd say yes. But that's as far as it goes.*

I wish she'd just come out and say, "Actually, the two of us are going out." That'd make it easier for me to accept.

Actually, doesn't it bother everyone else? Like, they've got to have noticed by now, right? That something fishy's going on between Merry and Kuzaku? Like, it's plain to see, isn't it? Or does everyone else just not care? Maybe I just care a little too much?

Maybe I'm just horny? Haruhiro wondered, half-mocking himself. *Horny. If I said I was like a wild beast in heat, that'd be too blatant. I feel like that's not quite it anyway. What is it then? I want to be in love? To have a girlfriend? Yeah, maybe that's it.*

I want a girlfriend.

...Not that I could get one.

"Yeah, this is the place," Haruhiro said. "This is the mineshaft."

Haruhiro looked to each of his comrades. He thought, *I want to dropkick Ranta. But other than that, my current party is more precious to me than anything.*

"But there's a hole now," Haruhiro said. "I dunno why. The question is, what do we do about it?"

Now's not the time to be saying that I want a girlfriend. When I think about Moguzo, somehow, I feel like it might be too early for me, too. I don't meet a lot of new people, so it's not like I have options. Besides, if I let my heart get distracted by silly things and have my head in the clouds, that'd be a big problem. I've got to keep myself together.

"It could be a new discovery," Haruhiro concluded.

When Haruhiro said that, his comrades, and Ranta in particular, got excited.

A discovery.

Someone must have discovered the Wonder Hole in the first place. Then, as exploration had progressed, there had been further discoveries inside the Wonder Hole, which continued to this day.

For instance, Soma, the head of the group Haruhiro and the others were, technically, members of, the Day Breakers, was always exploring uninhabited lands to find a route to the former kingdoms of Ishmal and Nanaka. He and his party were discovering unknown places and creatures every day.

Fundamentally, the glory of new discoveries would go to parties like Soma's, which were always pushing deeper and deeper. However, the Wonder Hole was infinitely vast. It was said that even the valley of holes, the muryan nest, and the kingdom of devils hadn't been fully explored, especially since natural disasters or the actions of the creatures that resided in it could cause the Wonder Hole to change at times. There was no way to anticipate where those changes might happen.

In other words, even Haruhiro and his party had a chance of making a new discovery. This hole could very well be it. On the other side of this hole, there might be a whole other world that nobody knew anything about.

"What do we do about it? Man—" Ranta licked his lips. "I don't even need to say it, do I? There's only one thing to do."

"I have a bad feeling..." Shihoru clutched her staff close, shrinking into herself and trembling.

"Is it my fault?!" Ranta shouted. "Is it my fault, huh, saggy tits?!"

"I told you, they're *not* saggy!" Shihoru shouted.

"And I told you, show me!"

"Oh...?" a voice said.

"Huh?" Haruhiro furrowed his brow.

Who had that "Oh...?" just now come from? It had been a guy's voice. But not Ranta's, or Kuzaku's.

Haruhiro turned around. He could see a light from a lantern or a similar piece of lighting equipment.

Someone was coming their way from the direction of the kingdom of the devils. Not just one person. He couldn't tell the exact number, but it was a party.

"Ah!" another man shouted.

"Huh?" Haruhiro reacted with surprise. This time, it was a voice he recognized.

Someone rushed out of the unfamiliar party and ran over to them.

"Hey, hey! Harucchi! If it isn't my ol' pal, Harucchi! What a dinky-coink! Oh, was that one too hard to get?! I mean a coinkydink, a coincidence! And what a coincidence it is, us meeting up here! It's me, me, little ol' me! Kikkawa! Yay, yay! Let's have a rah-hoo for

chance encounters! Get it?"

They had met up with Kikkawa.

Grimgar
of
Fantasy and Ash

2. The Clear Line Between Those Who Are Ordinary and Those Who Are Not

Haruhiro had come to Grimgar, probably without warning, in a group of eleven men and women.

There'd been Ranta, Shihoru, Yume, and the late Manato and Moguzo. There had also been Renji, Ron, Sassa, Adachi, and Chibi-chan.

And then there had been Kikkawa.

"Man, I mean, like, seriously! What a coinky-dinky-dink! Right?!" Kikkawa cried. "Meeting in a place like this—it's, like, priceless! I mean, seriously?! I'm pur-sized, sur-prized! Wow! Fantastic! Yay!"

He was abnormally easygoing, positive beyond reason, too energetic, gregarious as all get-out... He had connections everywhere and seemed to be the living embodiment of the word "frivolous."

Renji had quickly brought Ron, Sassa, Adachi, and Chibi-chan under his control and formed Team Renji, and now there was hardly a volunteer soldier who didn't know that name. They never seemed out of their depth, and had risen up to become a real force to be reckoned with.

As for Haruhiro and his group, they were the leftovers who had somehow managed to form a party and drag themselves along this far.

Kikkawa had been left on his own, and though it wasn't clear to Haruhiro how—he'd explained it once, but even then it hadn't made much sense—he'd managed to join one of the senior volunteer soldier parties. Since then, he'd been enjoying the volunteer soldier life with laughter and an excess of good cheer.

Kikkawa kept on babbling along. "Huh? So? What, what? Ohh, ohh, Ranta, how've you been? Shihoru, you're the same as ever, I see, I see, heh heh, no, I don't remember what's the same as ever, but, hey, Yume! Yumeeee! Yayyyy! You good?! Merry! Merry-chaaaan! Wow, you're even more beautiful than usual today—just kidding! Well, it's true, though! Kuzaku, right? You're huge, I mean, like, seriously! So? What, what, what? What're you all doing here? Playing around? Like, wanna play? In the Wonder Hole! Are you a bunch of players?! Wah ha ha ha ha!"

"Too noisy, yeah!" a petite, blonde-haired, blue-eyed girl called, putting her hand on Kikkawa's face and shoving. "Kikkawa's too noisy, yeah! Speaks too much, yeah!"

"Owow, owowowowow, wait, Anna-san, stop! Not the face! My face is important! It's my life!" Kikkawa howled.

"It's not a very *good* face, yeah! It's normal, yeah! It looks like shiitake mushroom, yeah?! It's bad, bad face, yeah?!" Anna-san snapped.

With Anna-san suddenly turning to them for agreement, Haruhiro stuttered a bit, not sure what to say, but Ranta was clutching his belly and laughing.

"Gyah ha ha ha! Shiitake! A shiitake, she says! Well, it's pretty normal, yeah, Kikkawa! Your face! I don't think it's a bad face, though! Well, maybe a bit below average!"

"Hey, bullshit!" Anna suddenly turned to Ranta and flipped him the bird. "What you insult our Kikkawa for?! *Kill you! Fuck you!"* she shouted in a mixture of broken speech and foreign expletives.

"...But, you said it first..." Ranta whined.

"Shut up! Anna-san say it? *Okay!* You say it? *No!* Figure that much out, warty-assed human!"

"Ha ha ha! I dunno what to say." Kikkawa was embarrassed for some reason. "Anna-san's love for me's, like, heavyweight class. It's a real KO show. Ha ha ha, bwah...?!"

"You dummy!" Anna-san hit Kikkawa with a straight right punch and KO-ed him for real. "There's no love there! It's like scorched earth! Anna-san *not love, but like,* yeah! How can you misunderstand?!"

Shihoru, Yume, Merry, Kuzaku—yes, Haruhiro, too, and even Ranta—were all overwhelmed by Anna-san's intensity.

By the way, Anna-san was wearing a priest's uniform with blue lines. Unbelievably, she was a priest. More than that, from what Haruhiro had heard, she'd been a mage before, too. It made no sense.

"Well, that aside—" An awfully pleasant and handsome man stepped forward. The handsome man wore a suit of armor with a hexagram engraved in it. He was a paladin, like Kuzaku. When he smiled, they caught a glimpse of his teeth. They sparkled white. He was, like, 200% handsome, and it was clear to see that he was the leader of the party Kikkawa had joined. "What were you up to here, Harukawa?"

"...No, um, my name's Haruhiro, Tokimune-san," Haruhiro said awkwardly. "I think I've corrected you on that twice."

"Oh, sorry, sorry," said Tokimune. "You're Kikkawa's pal, so maybe I figured you were connected by the kawa in your names, or something like that?"

"I'd appreciate it if, maybe, you wouldn't make that sort of connection between us...?" ventured Haruhiro.

"All right," Tokimune gave him a thumbs up, winking. "Haruhiro. I've got it now. Won't get it wrong again. I swear."

"...Sure."

You said the same thing while striking the same pose the last two times. But that was something Haruhiro decided not to say. *It's probably just how the guy is. After all, he let Kikkawa join his party, and they get along, so there's no way he's normal. Anna-san's got a pretty unique personality, too. Actually, the others are all pretty incredible.*

Though, it wasn't as if none of them looked *normal.*

"Well, you know," said a guy who looked sane, adjusting his glasses. He looked good in his priest uniform, too. The bulky warhammer he carried left some room for concern, but few people who were just passing by would look at him and think, *Oh, yeah, that guy's bad news.* "It's the mineshaft, so they've gotta be aiming for grimbles. Can't be anything else."

"Heh..." The tall man who grunted in response, on the other hand, was clearly bad news. First of all, he had a ponytail. Also, an eyepatch. And he was an old guy. He looked to be in his mid-to-late thirties, but they'd learned he wasn't actually *that* old. A quiver of arrows was slung over his back, and two one-edged swords hung at his hip. He wore a close-fitting leather jumpsuit, which made him look like, well... some kind of pervert. "The same as us, then... Huh. Heh..."

The one wearing glasses was Tada. The one with the eyepatch was

Inui. And there was one other person in Tokimune's party.

The last person in his party was a match for Inui when it came to height. If you included the mage hat she wore, she might have been taller than Inui. The mage's robe she wore wasn't that thick, but she still looked like she was bundled up in warm clothing.

She's huge, thought Haruhiro.

Of course, she wasn't as big as 190-centimeter-tall Kuzaku. Still, she was huge—for a woman, it might be sensible to add. But she was large enough that anyone who saw her would never forget her.

For all her height, the features of her face, rimmed by the thick, long hair which spilled out from under her mage hat, were small and understated. They looked like they belonged on a girl who was less than 160 centimeters tall.

Her name—what was it again? Haruhiro wondered. *I recognize her perfectly, but I can't quite remember. I know her nickname is Giantess.*

Ms. Giantess had eyes like a cute little animal, which suited her face but not her giant size, and they were fixated on Haruhiro for some reason.

No, that's not it, he realized. *It must be something behind me. Ms. Giantess must be staring at the hole.*

Haruhiro looked at Ranta.

...What do we do? he signaled Ranta with his eyes, looking for advice. Ranta always managed to figure out what he wanted, at least.

"Uh... Erm..." Ranta cleared his throat awkwardly, as he subtly moved to stand right in front of the hole.

Yeah, no, that's not subtle at all, Haruhiro thought.

If anything, it would have been fair to say Ranta drew Tokimune and his party's attention to the hole. Ranta seemed to sense that himself.

"...Th-this is, well... Can you pretend you didn't see it?" Ranta asked.

"Yeah," Tokimune said with a nod and a grin. "That's not happening!"

"That wasn't here last time we came through, was it?" the glasses-wearing Tada said, rubbing his chin and tilting his head to the side.

"So? So?" Kikkawa dashed towards the hole. "Could it be? Could it, maybe, be? No way! Like, no way?! Have we got a discovery here?! Is that it?!"

"H-hold on!" Ranta stood in Kikkawa's way. "We got here first! It's our discovery!"

"Nuh-uh-uh-uh," Kikkawa said, clinging to Ranta. "That's not *faiiiir*. Don't be like that, Ranta! We're buds, right? What's mine is mine, and what's yours is mine, too. Yeah?"

"Like hell it is, pal!" Ranta yelled, brushing Kikkawa off. "Not a chance, moron! Everything in this world belongs to me, Ranta-sama, obviously!"

"Heh..." Inui, the one wearing an eyepatch, put his hand on his swords' hilts. "Too much greed could be the end of you, you know..."

"Y-y-y-you wanna go?! I'll take you, punk!" Ranta hollered.

"If you're fighting, leave the rest of us out of it," Shihoru said, distancing herself from him.

"H-heyyyyy?!" Ranta looked to Haruhiro and the others in the group.

As if they had planned it out in advance, Haruhiro and the others all refused to make eye contact.

"Ha ha ha!" Anna-san cackled, puffing her chest out. While she only stood maybe 155 centimeters tall, her chest was big. "Stupid Ranta! Not popular, yeah! Just the way he looks, yeah!"

"Shut your face! You freckled pipsqueak with big tits! I'll grope you!" Ranta shouted.

"Try it, if you think you can, yeah! Because Anna-san's minions butcher you first! You no talk about my freckles, idiot! I am sensitive about that, moron! Stand on your hands and suck your dick, *asshole!* Dummy, dummy, dummy! Dumb Ranta! Ahhhh, no forgiveness! Punish him in name of heaven, yeah!"

"...Hey," Haruhiro gestured towards Ranta with his chin. "Apologize, Ranta. Anna-san's crying a bit."

"Why should I have to apologize?!" Ranta screamed. "Don't be ridi—"

"Hmm..." Tokimune patted Anna-san on the head, drawing his sword as he did. "Well, maybe I'll punish you in the name of heaven. We don't let anyone get away with hurting Anna-san. She's our precious mascot, after all."

"I...!" Ranta got down on his hands and knees at light speed. "I'm sorry?! I'll never mention the freckles again, so forgive me! Please?!"

"That was fast..." Ms. Giantess muttered to herself, taken aback.

"You dim-witted pumpkin-head!" Anna-san shouted, grinding her foot into the back of Ranta's head. "If you going to apologize, never say thing in first place! If you learn your lesson, you be Anna-san's slave starting today! Be grateful, *motherfucker!*"

Ranta groaned in pain as she stepped on his head, but he sat there and took it.

Well, it's probably best that he just takes it, Haruhiro thought. *If he doesn't restrain himself, things'll get out of hand.*

The biggest group of jokesters in the Volunteer Soldier Corps. That was the reputation that Tokimune's party, the Tokkis, had earned for themselves. But they'd been at this much longer than Haruhiro and his group. They had to be decent if they'd been active for that long.

The Tokkis weren't the type to play it safe, either. They were more than happy to take risks, and they'd still managed to keep going this long. They were more than just a group of eccentric jokesters.

Haruhiro had no intent of picking a fight with the Tokkis. Kikkawa had enlisted at the same time as them, and they owed him for introducing Merry to the party, too. If they could get along peaceably, he felt that would be for the best.

The problem was, did Tokimune feel the same way?

"Um, Tokimune-san," Haruhiro said.

"What is it, Haruhikawa?" Tokimune asked.

"...It's Haruhiro."

"Oh, my bad. So? What is it?" Tokimune sheathed his sword. "You wanna do it? Together. We'd be down with that."

That pleasant smile felt disconcerting now.

Do it. Together, Haruhiro thought. *Is that... our only option?*

Given the circumstances, it wouldn't be strange for the Tokkis, as their seniors, to ignore Haruhiro and the others, or push them aside, and take the discovery for themselves. *We won't do that—let's share the discovery,* was what Tokimune was proposing.

Well, we found the hole first, was something Haruhiro did feel, to some degree, but it wasn't a bad deal.

If they were happy just to be the ones who discovered it, that would be one thing. But, since they were here already, he wanted to explore it, too. The vast majority of volunteer soldiers had more experience and were more accomplished than Haruhiro and his party, but it was possible no one had ever gone past this point. If they could be the first to leave their own footprints here, he wanted to.

Yet, he had no idea what might be, or live, on the other side of the hole. It could be something, or someone, really, *really* dangerous, so there were risks.

If the Tokkis came with us, that would be reassuring, he thought. *If we can trust them, that is.*

"I have a condition, you could say..." Haruhiro said, carefully gauging Tokimune's expression.

Tokimune wore a pleasant smile, his white teeth peeking out.

Is he simply being open with us, or is he plotting something? Haruhiro wondered. *It's hard to get a grasp on this guy.*

"For the time being, at least, how about we keep this between us?" Haruhiro finished.

"That's fine," Tokimune said easily, giving him a thumbs up. "Haruhirokawa, until you and I talk it over, and we both give the go sign, it'll be a secret between the twelve of us here. Well, it's not like we can seal the area off, so if someone finds out, there's not much we can do."

"...Well, yeah, you're right about that," said Haruhiro. "It didn't seem like anyone but us had been coming to the mineshaft lately, but then you guys turned up, after all. Also, my name isn't Haruhirokawa, it's Haruhiro."

"Haruhiro, huh. Sorry, sorry. Hmm. Well, you know how it is. It was pure coincidence. Who was it that suggested we come here?"

"Me." Ms. Giantess raised her hand.

"Oh, yeah. Mimori, huh," Tokimune said, smiling far more than made any sense. "Mimori, why was it again? That we came to the mineshaft."

"Because I like grimbles," Ms. Giantess, whose name was apparently Mimori, said plainly. "They're cute."

"Right, right. That was it. I remember now, Mimori, you were saying you wanted to catch one to keep as a pet."

Mimori nodded.

...*Yep,* Haruhiro thought. *I knew Ms. Giantess would be a weirdo, too.*

"Aaaanyways." Tokimune stretched his right hand out towards Haruhiro. "Nice working with you, Haruhiro. Let's give it our all."

It looks like he finally learned my name, Haruhiro thought.

He glanced over at his comrades. Nobody seemed unhappy about it. Ranta was being stepped on by Anna-san, though.

"We're in your care," Haruhiro said, taking Tokimune's hand. "Take it easy on us."

"Heh heh heh!" Tokimune shook his hand up and down vigorously. "That could be a bit difficult, you know?"

3. Path to the Unknown

The hole was about three meters across, so they decided to advance down it two by two

The Tokkis would be led by Tokimune, the paladin, followed by Kikkawa, the warrior. Anna-san, the priest who had formerly been a mage, would come next, and the glasses-wearing Tada, the priest who'd previously been a thief. After them would be Mimori the Giantess, the mage who'd once been a warrior, and finally, eyepatch-wearing Inui, who had changed jobs from thief to warrior to hunter.

For Haruhiro's group, Haruhiro would take point, followed by Kuzaku the tank, Ranta, Shihoru, Merry, and Yume in that order.

Haruhiro, Tokimune, Shihoru, Inui, and Yume would each carry lanterns at the front, middle, and rear of the group, maintaining the minimum necessary level of light.

Once their marching order was determined, Tokimune headed right into the hole. "Well, let's get a move on."

"W-w-wait, Tokimune-san, that's not..." Haruhiro hurried after him. It looked like the man really had no intention of holding back.

The hole went straight. For now, it was just a hole. They didn't sense anything living in it. There didn't seem to be anything there.

They continued for maybe fifteen, twenty meters like that. Then they hit a wall.

"Oh," Tokimune kicked the wall in front of them lightly, as if pushing it with his foot. "Looks like the path splits here, huh?"

"You're right." Haruhiro moved the lantern left, then right. "Right or left, huh?"

"Which do you prefer, Haruhiro?" Tokimune asked.

"Come again?"

"Right or left?"

"Huh? We're splitting up?" Haruhiro asked.

"Huh? Why wouldn't we? After we were lucky enough to find a fork in the road?"

"Err..." said Haruhiro.

I don't understand. Haruhiro wasn't tired at all, but he rubbed his eyes. *This guy's thought process, or mode of thinking, or whatever it is—I don't get it. I can't keep up. If we have two parties working together, wouldn't it be better not to split up? If we all stick together, it's got to be safer that way.*

"It's gotta be left!" Ranta shouted. "Left is the one that suits me best! I'm sure of it!"

I don't understand him, either. Haruhiro had no idea why left would suit Ranta better. Not that he cared.

"Gotcha." Tokimune gave him a thumbs up. "We'll go right, then."

The words had scarcely left his mouth before Tokimune and the Tokkis headed down the right-hand path. One of them was even humming a little tune.

It's probably the glasses-wearing Tada, Haruhiro thought. *Yeah, he looks sane, but he's a weirdo, too. His history as a warrior-turned-priest was kind of weird already...*

"Let's go, too!" Ranta bellowed.

Ranta was in high spirits. Or, to be precise, only Ranta was in high spirits.

Haruhiro sighed. *I bet I'll set a new record for number of sighs today. No, not that I've ever counted,* he thought.

"We're going to advance cautiously," he told his party.

"I'm in favor of that," Kuzaku said.

"I'm against it! Against! Against, you hear!" Ranta hollered.

Ranta, shut up, Haruhiro thought.

"It's fine takin' it nice and slow," said Yume. "Right, Shihoru? Merry-chan?"

"...Yeah," said Shihoru.

"I'd say so," Merry agreed.

"Majority is in favor, then," Haruhiro said, sighing to get himself back in the right mindset. "Ranta, shut up for a bit."

"No way," snapped Ranta. "I'd sooner die than be quiet, scum."

"Yeah, whatever..." Haruhiro muttered.

Paying him no further mind, Haruhiro used Sneaking to progress down the left path. The lanterns were his only source of light. When it was this dark, he relied more on his ears than his eyes. It seemed like Ranta at least understood that much, so he didn't open his mouth.

It's three meters across, the same as before, Haruhiro thought. *Two meters tall, too. That's about the same. I wouldn't quite call the ground smooth; it's bumpy, but not enough that it makes it hard to walk. The walls are like that, too.*

This isn't a naturally formed hole. It's clear that someone dug it out. That means there must be something in here.

The path is gently curving to the right now...

"Boo!" Ranta-the-idiot suddenly shouted.

"Eek!"

"Mrrrow?!"

"Eep!" shrieked Shihoru.

The girls all screamed, causing Ranta to laugh like an idiot.

"Gwohyehhyehhyeh. Don't be a bunch of chickens!"

"G-geez!" Yume cried tearfully. "That was really startlin'! Stupid! Stupid Ranta!"

"If only he'd just die," Shihoru muttered in a frightening tone.

"O light, may Lumiaris's divine protection be upon you..." Merry made the sign of the hexagram. "Lay a curse on Ranta."

"Like that'd even work! I'm totally fine!" Ranta declared with a cackling laugh.

"I have to respect the guy, in a way," Kuzaku said, smiling just a little.

"Wait, hold on..." Haruhiro said, sighing. "Ranta, just summon Zodiac-kun. You're useless—no, worse than useless—at this stuff, but Zodiac-kun'll at least tell us if there's something coming... If it feels like it, that is."

"What's with the condescending attitude?" Ranta demanded. "Beg me to do it. 'Please summon Zodiac-kun, Ranta-sama, I'm begging you.' Bow your head and say it like that."

"If Zodiac-kun were here, we wouldn't be needin' you," said Yume. "Little wonder you don't want to summon it. Since it renders your existence meaningless and all."

"As if," Ranta snapped. "Fine. If you're gonna be so insistent, why don't I summon it? Let me tell you, though. Zodiac-kun's no more than a part of me, and it'll only do as I say. If you want Zodiac-kun to do any work, you'd better do as I tell you to. You got that, you losers? O darkness, O Lord of Vice, Demon Call!"

In front of Ranta, something like a blackish, purplish cloud appeared. The clouds whirled into a vortex, taking on a familiar shape. It had a form like a person with a purple sheet thrown over their head, with two holes for eyes. Beneath the holes, there was a gash-like mouth. In its right hand, there was something like a carving knife, while in its left hand, it held a club-like object.

Dread knight Ranta's demon familiar, Zodiac-kun, had been much cuter in its previous incarnation. Even if it was no Anna-san, it had been mascot-like.

Zodiac-kun had changed when Ranta had accumulated enough vice. Now, the demon's form was more human, and it had legs that were strangely detailed, complete with thighs, knees, calves, ankles, and feet, despite it floating all the time. Honestly, it was adorably gross, or maybe just gross.

"...Kehe... Kehehehe... Don't call me, Ranta, you turd... Suffer for a thousand years and then die..."

"What? *That's* what I get right off the bat?!" Ranta screamed.

Weird as Zodiac-kun looked, it was always quick to insult and put down Ranta, which Haruhiro and the others enjoyed seeing.

"We're counting on you, Zodiac-kun," Haruhiro called out.

Zodiac-kun nodded its head without responding. The demon made a policy of not talking to anyone but its dread knight, apparently.

"Wah ha ha ha," Ranta laughed at that. "You got ignored. Take that!"

"...Ehehe... Ehe... Haruhiro..." the demon cackled.

"Huh?" Haruhiro said. It was the first time the demon had called him by name, so he was surprised. When he looked back, Zodiac-kun was turned to face Haruhiro.

"...You live... Kehe... Kehehehehe... Ranta can die... Kehehehe..."

"Gauuun!" Ranta made a strange sound effect. That one must have shocked him pretty badly.

"Zodiac-kun, you're a good kid!" Yume rushed over and rubbed Zodiac-kun's back.

"...Kehe... Kehehehe... Kehe... Kehehe..." Zodiac-kun was trying to turn its face away from Yume, but it seemed happy.

"...D-d-damn it...!" Ranta had fallen to the ground and was gnashing his teeth. "Zodiac-kun's supposed to belong to me, and me alone! You're not the Zodiac-kun I know anymore!"

"...Ehehe... Ranta..."

"What, Zodiac-kun...? It's a little late! I don't want to hear you beg for my forgiveness!"

"...Look... Kehehe... They like me... Kehehehe... Unlike you..."

"Guaughhhhhh...?!" Ranta wailed.

Nice one, Zodiac-kun, Haruhiro thought. Zodiac-kun might be the only one capable of accurately landing attacks on Ranta's psyche.

Thanks to Zodiac-kun, Haruhiro felt a little better now. For all the abuse, though, the demon would do everything it could to protect Ranta sometimes. It seemed that the accuracy of the warnings it would whisper to Ranta when it sensed impending danger were increasing with his accumulated vice. Still, it was a capricious creature, so as long as they didn't rely on it too much, it could be a big help.

The path keeps curving to the right, Haruhiro thought as they moved forward. *There's no incline. The height and width haven't changed. I don't sense anyone else here.*

...No.

Up ahead, I can see something.

Haruhiro gulped.

"Light?" he said aloud.

"You think something's there?" Kuzaku put his hand on the hilt of his sword.

"...Get ready for battle?" Yume asked in a whisper.

Phew, he heard Merry exhale. She had probably just checked the glowing hexagram on her left wrist. Protection hadn't worn off yet.

"They here? They here, they here?" Ranta licked his lips. "They finally, finally here? What's the enemy like?"

"...Kehehehe... These enemies... Ranta... Are going to kill you... Kehehehehe..."

"Listen, Zodiac kun, if I die, you disappear too, you got that?" Ranta snarled.

"But...isn't that..." Shihoru seemed to have figured it out.

That's right.

Haruhiro called out. "Tokimune-san!"

"Hey," came the immediate reply.

The light came from their lanterns.

When they moved forward, the Tokkis were all there waiting for them. To sum up what had happened, when they'd gone in through the first hole, it had split left and right. Those two paths had formed a circle and met here.

However, it was too soon to be disappointed. There was more to come.

"Left or right, it was all the same, huh?" Tada said, his glasses flashing. Well, actually, they just looked like they flashed because of the way the lantern light reflected off of them.

"It look like this, yeah," Anna-san said proudly, holding up an open notebook.

There was something scribbled inside. It looked like a warped circle, but with short, crooked lines coming up and down off it.

"Erm..." Haruhiro hesitantly looked Anna-san in the eye. "What's this?"

"A map, yeah!" yelled Anna-san. "What else it *look* like?! Wait, you people don't draw maps?! Useless!"

"We came in here, and..." Kikkawa first pointed to the crooked line going down, and then pointed to the line going up where the warped circle met, "...here's where we are now! Nice going, Anna-san! It's a perfect map!"

"What's so perfect about it?" Ranta complained, looking disappointed.

This one time, Haruhiro had to agree with Ranta—but, obviously, he kept quiet.

"Dumb Ranta is dumb so can't read maps, yeah," taunted Anna-san. "Dummy, dummy."

"The eye of the heart..." Inui said with a slight smile as he adjusted his eyepatch. "You have to read Anna-san's maps with the eye of the heart... Heh..."

No, that makes no sense, Haruhiro thought. *And, wait, you call her Anna-san with a -san, too?*

I have a mountain of things I want to say. But I'm not gonna. I'll only be subjecting myself to more nonsense if I do. I just have to get used to it, Haruhiro thought. *Is this something you can get used to...?*

"For now, let's get going, Okay?" Tokimune gave them a thumbs up with one eye closed.

"Oh, sure, sounds good..." Haruhiro said.

Better hurry, or we'll get left behind, he thought. *I'm not so sure I'd mind being left behind at this point, but, no, no, no, we just got started exploring. Besides, we haven't found anything interesting yet.*

They continued moving forward in two columns, like before, when Haruhiro noticed the path sloped. They were on a smooth downward incline.

"It's sloping down, right?" Haruhiro asked.

"Sure is." Tokimune seemed to be enjoying himself. "I've got a good feeling. Like there ought to be something soon."

Here's hoping, Haruhiro thought. *So long as it's not dangerous.*

The incline grew steeper, then the path took a hard turn to the left. From there, it gently bent leftwards. It was still a downwards slope.

"Anna-san," the glasses-wearing Tada suddenly said. "You think you can hold your bladder?"

"I-i-i-i-i-it fine! Not going to wet myself anymore, yeah?!"

"...So she's done it before," Kuzaku whispered.

"*L-li'l bit!* Just a little, yeah! One time only, okay?!"

"Gehehehe!" Ranta laughed vulgarly. "Wetting yourself! What are you, a little kid?!"

"Curly-kun," Tokimune laughed and without turning around, said, "did I not tell you not to hurt our Anna-san?"

"S-sorry! I'll be careful! Won't happen again!" Ranta said

immediately.

"...Kehe... Actually... get cut to ribbons... Ranta... Kehehehehe..."

"Y'know, maybe," Yume giggled, "it'd be worth leavin' Ranta with the Tokkis for a while. Then he'd quiet down a bit, don't you think?"

"Why settle for 'a while'? Let them have him forever," Shihoru said with a smirk.

"Yeah," Merry coldly agreed.

"Aw, man." Kikkawa snapped his fingers for some reason. "I dunno about that. We don't really want him, y'know? I mean, you know what Ranta's like? I think he's an amusing guy, but...what can I say? He's the kind of guy who's best when, like, you only see him once in a while?"

"We don't want him." Mimori the Giantess bluntly shot down the idea.

"Oh, shut up! I don't want to be part of your stupid party, either!" Ranta hollered.

"...Ehe... Ehehe... Don't let it get you down... Ehehehe... Ranta..."

"Z-Zodiac-kun, buddy...are you trying to comfort me?"

"...Remember... Kehe... The whole world hates you... This shouldn't be enough to get you down..."

"*That's* why?!" Ranta shouted.

Ugh, he's so annoying, Haruhiro thought. He hadn't let his guard down yet...as far as he himself was concerned. He couldn't help but worry if he was doing enough, but it was hard to maintain focus. *Don't blame me if this all goes south, okay?*

Eventually, they came to another fork in the path.

Straight and right, Haruhiro noted. *Guess we're splitting up again...*

But Tokimune said something else. "First, we'll try going straight. All together."

"...Huh?" Haruhiro said, startled. "Sure. Is that what you want to do?"

"Yeah," the man said. "I feel like it's the right choice."

"Erm...any basis for that?" Haruhiro asked.

"Basis? Hmm." Tokimune flashed his white teeth at Haruhiro. "A hunch, I guess?"

Seriously? Haruhiro thought. *What's with that? It's pretty random. Ahh, I want to complain.*

But the Tokkis seemed to believe in Tokimune's judgment, and they immediately got themselves ready. Did that mean Tokimune's hunches were often on the mark? If so, Haruhiro considered perhaps trusting him, too.

When they went straight, they came out into an oblong room. Maybe it wasn't so much a room as a section of tunnel that was wider, so it felt a bit like a room—no, there was more to it than that.

"Here it is, Haruhiro." Tokimune gleefully slapped Haruhiro on the back. "This is what I'm talking about. You've gotta have stuff like this."

"Wh-what is that thing?" Haruhiro stammered.

The wall, and the ground near the wall—those aren't rocks, they're mysterious objects. They're...clinging to it...maybe? There are a lot of them. Enough that I don't feel like counting. They're about 30 centimeters big? Or bigger? They might be 50 centimeters, maybe more. They're round, and shine a little. Blue, green, yellow—they're glowing faintly in a variety of colors. Almost like they're pulsating.

"You know..." Ranta's voice was uncharacteristically low. "...It's like...they're alive, isn't it? Somehow..."

"You ever seen this before?" Haruhiro checked with Tokimune, just to be sure.

"Never," Tokimune said clearly. "Not once. Nothing like this. It's a fresh experience. Real fresh."

"...Ranta..." hissed the demon.

"Oh? What is it, Zodiac-kun?" Ranta asked. "What's up?"

"...Was just... seeing if you'd respond... Kehehehe..."

"What for?!" Ranta yelled.

Was Zodiac-kun *really* only seeing if he could get a response? He was capricious. Even when the demon was trying to tell them something, it rarely did so in a straightforward manner. It wouldn't hurt to stay cautious.

Those objects were also on the wall near the room's entrance. Haruhiro prepared to draw his dagger, looking at them closely.

There's a faint greenish light growing stronger and then dimming again, Haruhiro thought. *It's like they really are alive. They're, like, I dunno—like eggs. Eggs don't glow, though. But if you were to shine a light through an egg with a really, really thin shell, it might look like this.*

There's something like a shadow in the greenish light, he added silently. *The shadow seems to be moving.*

"What...do we do?" Haruhiro asked.

It was partly because he wanted to let his seniors look good, but Haruhiro was asking Tokimune what to do about everything. It might be better to show some independence.

"Want to try breaking them?" Tokimune suggested lightly.

"Huh?" Haruhiro asked.

"To see what's inside," the man said. "You want to check, right?"

Tokimune drew his sword and immediately stabbed it into one of the nearby glowing things. They were apparently not that hard.

There was a wet, squelching sound. The thick, oozy contents flowed out. Tokimune cut away the shell, stirring the insides with his sword.

"Oh!" he cried.

It looked like he'd caught something. Tokimune twisted his wrist and fished whatever-it-was out. It fell to the ground through the hole he had torn open. With a wet thud, it landed on the ground.

Everyone was holding their breath.

Tokimune crouched down, illuminating it with his lantern.

It was still moving, though only slightly. It resembled a mammalian fetus, perhaps 15 centimeters long.

It stopped moving.

It's dead...maybe, Haruhiro thought.

"Wonder what it is." Tokimune looked to his sword, now thoroughly covered in ooze. "It's a creature of some sort, that much is clear. Think they're eggs, after all? Like, this is a spawning ground of sorts?"

"There're a lot of them here, these eggs," the glasses-wearing Tada said with a snort. "If they all hatch, we're in for some fun times."

"Eggs. Okay..." Anna-san was drawing in the notebook that was apparently her book of maps with a serious expression on her face.

Mimori the Giantess crouched down next to Tokimune. She was staring at the fetus-like creature's remains.

"You want one as a pet?" Tokimune asked.

"Not so much," Mimori shook her head. "Are they tasty?"

"Heh..." The eye not covered by Inui's eyepatch suddenly flared open. "Like we should know!"

This guy suddenly snapped at her, Haruhiro thought, surprised.

Was it really something to get upset over? I don't get this guy at all. He's scary.

No, but, the fetus-like creatures and their eggs are way scarier.

"Wanna smash all of them?" Kikkawa asked, as easily as he might suggest taking a short break.

"There're too many." Ranta looked around the room. "How many do you think there are? We'd be at it all day."

"...Kehehe... Ranta... You're actually sounding reasonable... You're going to die soon... Kehehehe..."

"Don't jinx me like that!" Ranta yelled.

"Ranta's right on this one." Tokimune stood up and shrugged his shoulders. "It's too much trouble to smash them all. I mean, they don't look like they'll hatch for a while anyway? Probably not a threat... Not *these* ones, anyway. Not yet."

4. For Now, We Just Look Towards Tomorrow

"...Ahh..." Haruhiro laid his head down on the small table and closed his eyes.

The Lonesome Field Outpost's back streets were a place for shopping, entertainment, and also the residential quarter. A number of the stalls stayed open quite late into the night, and Haruhiro had made the one with the least customers, a place that was always gloomy and mostly empty, into his regular haunt.

Well, it was little wonder the place wasn't more popular: the food was awful, and the drinks were average. The owner always looked grumpy, and wasn't the welcoming sort.

There were five seats at the counter, as well as another two tables in front of the stall, each of which had three chairs.

Tonight, there was one customer at the counter. Other than that, it was just Haruhiro at one of the tables. In other words, there were only two customers. That was still more than usual. It wasn't uncommon for Haruhiro to have the place to himself.

Obviously, around dinner time, there would be a few more people, but the place was more or less always like this when it got later into the night. It wasn't really any of his business, but, honestly, Haruhiro thought the owner would be better off to just close up shop a bit earlier.

Haruhiro would be nursing a glass of wine or a beer he didn't even want to drink as he fought off his sleepiness—until it finally overcame him. No matter how you looked at it, he wasn't a good customer.

"I'm beat..." Haruhiro mumbled.

It was an awful stall, but it had its good points. Even when Haruhiro started mumbling to himself like this, he didn't have to worry that anyone would hear him. If he nodded off, the owner would leave him be.

He could be by himself.

If he were alone all the time, he'd probably get lonely. But here at the Lonesome Field Outpost, they were living in a tent, which meant he was with Ranta, Kuzaku, or both, at pretty much all times. When he went into the Wonder Hole, of course, that was with his comrades, too, so he had hardly any time to himself.

The only chance he had for it was coming here like this, deliberately making that time for himself.

"...Well, it's fine," he mumbled.

It wasn't like he didn't complain, didn't vent his dissatisfaction at all. He made a point of saying as much as he ought to say, because holding it all in wouldn't do any good.

But there were some things he ought not to say, and things that couldn't be fixed no matter what he said about them. There were things that, in the end, he had to keep to himself.

"If it's between comrades...that's still not so bad...but if it's about other people..." Haruhiro was thinking it was best not to air his uncertainties about their joint exploration with the Tokkis, or to badmouth them to his comrades.

No one had opposed the decision, but it was still Haruhiro who had made the decision to work with the Tokkis. It would be unmanly to grumble about it now. Besides, if Haruhiro voiced an unfavorable opinion of the Tokkis, that would influence his comrades in some small way. Haruhiro was afraid to create an atmosphere where the others started to feel, *The Tokkis suck. We can't keep on going like this.*

It's still just the first day, Haruhiro told himself. *It's only natural that we're not working together all that well yet. The Tokkis may be a bunch of weirdos, but they're not bad folks, and we'll have fun together— maybe. I think. I want to think that. I have to.*

Be positive. Optimistic. Forward-thinking. Or able to appear that way, at least.

"...Don't ask for the impossible..." Haruhiro mumbled. He looked up, taking a sip from his now-lukewarm beer.

It's just not who I am. Being positive, optimistic, forward-looking. If anything, I'm the opposite. I'm negative, cynical, and always stuck on the past.

"...That's it," he said. *I'm starting to understand.*

Tokimune seemed like an impulsive guy. He didn't think about things deeply, and he did whatever came to mind. He moved forward based on what seemed to him like it would work, and everyone followed. After that, it actually did work out.

But, even if it's worked out that way so far, that doesn't mean it always will, right? He could mess up, couldn't he? It'll be too late to do anything about it once he's already screwed up badly, so wouldn't it be better to be cautious? I'm scared. It's damn scary. Being a leader, I mean. He needs to do, I dunno, risk management, I guess? He needs to think about that sort of stuff. He's got to.

"No, that's not it…" Haruhiro murmured.

That's not what this is about. Well, no, it is what it's about, at least in part, but there's more to it.

"…Am I jealous?" he asked aloud. "Of people like Tokimune?"

They were the biggest party of jokesters in the Volunteer Soldier Corps. A gang of complete and utter weirdos. But it wasn't as if they had no talent. Tokmune was pulling along a party like that on intuition and momentum. From his attitude when it came to Anna-san, he seemed to care for his comrades, and they seemed to trust him as well.

Tokimune was a weirdo. Haruhiro was too plain and ordinary.

It wasn't that he *wanted* to be weird. It was just that, when he was next to a person like Tokimune, he started to feel a bit pathetic about his own mundanity.

To put it a bit more strongly, he felt inferior. Maybe that was making him more irritable than he needed to be.

"…Yeah. There's that. That's part of it. He's cool… The guy's cool…"

Haruhiro didn't know that many leaders. Offhand, he could think of Shinohara of Orion, Renji of Team Renji, Kajiko of the Wild Angels, Soma of the Day Breakers, and, finally, Tokimune of the Tokkis. That was about it.

When I list them like that, each of them is cool in their own way.

"…Is it charisma?" Haruhiro wondered.

Yeah. That's it. They have charisma. An aura that's all their own, something that makes them stand out. They feel different. I dunno if

they were always that way, but, really, I think they must have had an aptitude for it.

Maybe they were people who had something Haruhiro didn't.

He'd felt that way all along. He knew it to be true. Haruhiro couldn't be like Soma, obviously, or even Renji or Shinohara. Still, he had to be marginally better than Ranta, at least, and he couldn't push the job off on anyone else, so he'd have to do it. He'd managed to do it somehow, so far.

Haruhiro was trying as hard as he could, and he didn't think things like, *I want to be recognized for it,* or, *Give me a break already.*

"...Sorry..." Haruhiro buried his head in his arms again.

It's gonna be painful. I'm sorry I'm such a bad leader. He was starting to feel bad for his comrades. A more charismatic, decisive, capable leader might be able to make his comrades' strengths stand out more. Renji had tried to poach Ranta. Shihoru and Yume had received an offer from Kajiko. Haruhiro suspected that even Merry and Kuzaku ought to be able to do better than they were now. That perhaps he, as the party leader, was the bottleneck holding everyone back.

"...I wanna be cool..."

Haruhiro laughed.

Yeah, I can't say that.

I can't say that to anyone.

I have to hold onto it all by myself.

"...Okay."

Haruhiro sat up and polished off the rest of his beer in one go. He winced.

Disgusting. Why do I have to drink this awful swill? He often thought that. Yet, still he drank it. It was a mystery why.

He left his ceramic mug on the counter.

"Thanks."

Of course, the owner, his face half-hidden behind a bushy beard, only cast a glance in Haruhiro's direction, not saying anything.

A "Thank you for your business," or a "Come again." Say that much, at least. Haruhiro thought that every time. Yet, still he came to this place. But, maybe I should stop. He'd thought this a number of times now, too.

He walked slowly through the back streets.

They had managed to wrap up their exploration for the day safely. It'd been a first-time experience, so he didn't know if it had gone well or not. Regardless, as they'd progressed down the path, there had been more of those wide rooms with the faintly glowing egg-like objects in them. They had searched ten rooms of roughly the same width before turning back, and he felt like he'd be stuck looking at those eggs in more of those wide rooms tomorrow.

He felt like, Is that all? But at the same time, there was a unique sense of tension and anticipation, so it was fun in a way. If they encountered a creature no one had ever seen before, that'd get him pretty fired up. But that excitement would probably come with an equal measure of terror.

He didn't want to lose anyone the way they'd lost Manato and Moguzo.

Though, now, he didn't feel the same pain he did back then. If anything, he noticed that he was beginning to forget the pain. If this kept up, he might repeat the same mistakes. That was scary, too.

I can't talk about this, either.

When Haruhiro talked with his comrades, Manato and Moguzo's

names never came up.

Was that intentional? It might be something he was doing unconsciously. Either way, he was avoiding the topic.

"...What a pain." Haruhiro stopped walking and looked up into the night sky.

He couldn't whine in front of his comrades. Was he trying to look cool? As leader, he didn't want to show any weakness. He couldn't make his comrades worry. Couldn't get careless. Couldn't do this, that, or the other thing. He couldn't do anything. Gotta do this thing. Oughta do that thing. And even after forcing himself to try so hard, he was always going to be ordinary. He could only be an average leader, at best.

"It's just not fair, huh..." he mumbled.

I wish I at least had a girlfriend.

"No, that's, I dunno... Would I call what I want a girlfriend?" Haruhiro scratched his head vigorously.

What is it? Peace of mind? Someone I can speak openly with, in a fully trusting relationship? Or is it warmth? Well, maybe I want that, too. Like, wouldn't it be great to have someone to hug? Or more like someone to hug me, maybe?

"Aughhhhh... I'm gross... Ahhhh!" he burst out.

Oh, crap, he thought, appalled. *This isn't the bar. I'm in the middle of the street. What do I think I'm doing here?*

Haruhiro sensed someone stopping. He looked to see who it was, and... *Those two up ahead, huh.* He was struck by a slight bout of dizziness.

"Ohh..." the little one said.

The one next to the little one was huge. Had to be over 180

centimeters. Not just tall, but big in general, though not fat. Because the little one was small, they made an incredibly contrasting pair.

"What you *doing,* Haruhirokawa?" the little one asked.

"Nothing, really..." Haruhiro said, backing away. "...Nothing special..."

They're staring. They're staring at me. Staring hard. Especially, no, not Anna-san—it's the big one.

The giantess, Mimori, with those small, animal-like features of hers that were incongruous with her height, was staring *reeeeeally* hard at Haruhiro.

He wanted to run away, but that'd be awkward. It'd make them wonder what was wrong with him. He didn't want them, of all people, thinking he was the strange one.

"H-how about you two?" Haruhiro stuttered. "What are you up to, out so late?"

"It's walk, yeah," said Anna-san. "*Girls'* walk. It's *night walking,* yeah. Is Haruhirokawa on journey of self-discovery?"

"Ha ha," Haruhiro laughed awkwardly. "It's not like that. I'm not on a journey. No way. What's that supposed to be? What do you mean, self-discover...?"

"Aughhhhhh!" Anna-san started tearing at her hair, a horrifying look on her face. "I'm gwosssssh!"

"I didn't say 'gwosh,'" Haruhiro said, confused. "Wait, what is 'gwosh' even supposed to..."

"*Why?* Why you ask Anna-san, yeah? You the one who say it, you ringworm!"

"No, I said I'm gross..."

"Gross!" Anna-san pointed her finger at Haruhiro, laughing so hard she cried. "Gross! That word fit you like glove, yeah! Gross!"

"...You could be right." He didn't have the willpower to refute her—or, rather, he couldn't refute it.

Yeah, I'm lame, I know it. I'm plain, boring, indecisive, and gross. Yeah, yeah, you're right. That's exactly it.

"Well, anyway, it's night, so be careful," he said. "See you tomorrow."

Haruhiro turned around and went the other way. It was the opposite of the direction he needed to go to get back to the tent, but he could take the long way around.

As soon as he started walking, one of them immediately called after him.

"H-hey!"

"...Yes?" Haruhiro asked.

When he looked back, Anna-san was fidgeting awkwardly. "Uh... you know... um... J-Just now, too much... I go too far, maybe? Yeah? Yeah...?"

"Huh? What do you mean?" he asked, confused.

"...Uh... G-g-gross?"

"Ohh." He finally understood. Anna-san was apparently trying to apologize. Haruhiro smiled wryly.

It's no big deal, really. It didn't bother me that much.

"It's fine," he said. "Honestly, I think it's a fair thing to call me. I'm aware of that."

"No! Y-you not gross, yeah?" Anna-san raised the index finger of her right hand and shook it back and forth. "You not all that gross."

I'm not all that gross, huh? he thought, but it might have just been how she talked. She didn't seem to mean anything bad by it. He felt like he might understand, just a little, why Anna-san was treasured as the Tokkis' mascot. She had a foul mouth, and was loud too, but it was hard to hate her.

"Thank you," he said. "Well, anyway, I need to get back and sleep. Good night, Anna-san and Mimori-san."

When he bowed and turned to go, he was stopped again.

"Wait."

"...Yes?" Haruhiro asked, turning around again.

This time, it wasn't Anna-san. It was Mimori. And she was walking over to Haruhiro at a steady pace.

"Huh? Wha? Wha...?" he fumbled.

What? Am I about to get killed? Mimori's as expressionless as ever. But her intensity's incredible. I mean, she's huge.

Mimori came to a sudden stop right in front of Haruhiro's face. She was looking down at him. She had a good ten centimeters on him.

"Mimorin," said Mimori.

"Huh?" Haruhiro said, blinking while scared stiff. "...Mi? Mimo... Mimo...rin...?"

"*My God...*" Anna-san covered her mouth with her hands.

"Yes," Mimori nodded. "Mimorin."

"...Huh? What's that...?"

"My name."

"...Mimori-san?" he said.

"Call me Mimorin. From here on, that's what I want you to call me. Mimorin."

"...Mimorin?"

"Right."

"...S-sure," Haruhiro stuttered. "I...can do that. Mimorin."

"That's good." Mimorin narrowed her eyes, both corners of her

mouth rising. It was a smile. And a satisfied one, at that.

Mimorin made an about-face and took off. Anna-san chased after Mimorin, making a lot of noise about something.

"Mimorin! What the hell?! Are you crazy?!"

...Or something like that.

I don't get it. Haruhiro had no idea what to make of it. *Well, whatever. Is this okay? I'm not even sure, but I should get back and sleep.*

For tomorrow's sake.

Grimgar *of* Fantasy *and* Ash

5. The Best Person to Put in Charge of Raising Pets

At eight in the morning, everyone gathered at the Wonder Hole. They passed through the valley of holes, the muryans' nest, and the kingdom of devils to reach the problem spot.

Haruhiro and the others were, for convenience's sake, referring to it by the code name, NA. It wasn't a particularly inventive code name. It was a new and unexplored area, so the acronym stood for New Area.

It seemed that, so far at least, only Haruhiro's party and the Tokkis knew of the NA's existence. Or so he wanted to think.

When preparations like casting Protection and summoning Zodiac-kun were finished, they proceeded through the hole in double file, like the day before, proceeding down the round tunnels to check the oblong rooms.

They had already checked the first ten yesterday, so they only gave those a cursory inspection today. They showed no noticeable change, but glasses-wearing Tada noticed one thing.

"It's only by a bit each time, but the eggs are getting bigger the deeper we go," Tada commented.

"Now that you mention it, you could be right," Haruhiro said, turning to take a peek.

It seemed he wasn't imagining it. Haruhiro had noticed something else.

Someone had been watching him since morning.

It was Mimori—no, Mimorin.

But, well, all Mimorin was doing was looking at Haruhiro. She was expressionless, so it was impossible to tell what she was thinking, or rather, hard to imagine she was thinking anything at all. No, she had to be thinking something; she couldn't not be. She was human, after all.

Not that it mattered. It wasn't hurting Haruhiro any. She was just looking. He just had to not let it bother him. It did make him wonder, though, you know...?

"Hmm." Tokimune showed his white teeth. "I get it. That's a good trend, a good trend indeed. Well, I guess we'll move on to the eleventh room."

And so, Haruhiro and the others stepped into the eleventh room. He wasn't feeling tense at all until Zodiac-kun sounded the alarm.

"...Kehehe... Ranta... The shadow of death is coming... Kehehehe..."

"Huh? Cut it out with the ominous—" Ranta started to snap back at the demon as usual.

Tokimune stopped right before entering the room and Haruhiro stopped, too. They glanced to one another.

Everyone got ready for battle.

Haruhiro laid the lantern at his feet, trying not to make a sound. *I'll go look,* he signaled to Tokimune. Tokimune nodded.

Just to be prudent, Haruhiro drew his dagger and entered the eleventh room using Sneaking.

Because the ground wasn't completely flat, it was hard to use Sneaking here. It required considerable concentration. The hard part was that with the walls covered in glowing eggs, it was difficult to progress along the walls. Haruhiro lowered his posture as much as possible, walking as far from the light source as he could, in the center of the room where it was darkest. He looked at the egg-coated walls.

To my right.

Something's there.

Going by its build and figure, it's like a goblin. It's pressed up against the eggs and looking this way. It's scared...?

The creature had been doing something here when it'd detected Haruhiro and the others. It had wanted to run, but hadn't been able to, so it had stayed hidden, praying Haruhiro and the others wouldn't come into this room. However, Haruhiro had in fact come in, so now, it was cowering.

He could tell that.

"Hey," Haruhiro said.

The thing jumped a little and shook its head. It was apparently a real coward. But, that didn't necessarily mean it wasn't dangerous. It might have access to magic of some sort, for instance.

Gotta strike the first blow, Haruhiro thought. *That's the only option.*

"Everyone, get in here! We've got company!" he called.

The Tokkis piled into the room, followed by Kuzaku and Ranta.

The creature was still cowering. It made no sound.

Haruhiro shouted as he rushed towards it. "It's on the right! Don't kill it!"

"Haruhiroooo...!" Tokimune shouted.

When Haruhiro glanced back, Tokimune was throwing something. ...*Wait, is that a shield?*

"You're in the way! Get down!"

"Whoa!" Haruhiro got down, as ordered. Tokimune's shield sailed over the top of his head, spinning as it went.

It struck a solid blow. There was a painful-sounding impact, followed by a groan of pain, probably from the goblin-like creature.

Several people jumped over Haruhiro. By the time he got up, the Tokkis had surrounded that goblin-like creature.

The goblin-like creature wasn't dazed. It had fallen to the ground, both hands raised, as if to say, *I surrender.*

Inui crouched down, bringing the lantern up to its face. A goblin... it was not. Its face and its entire body resembled a bat.

"This guy's a real ri-komo, huh," Kikkawa said, having the same opinion as Haruhiro.

Ri-komo, Haruhiro thought, translating it. *Komori. He probably means a bat, I think.*

"Ohh," Tokimune sounded impressed. "Well, let's call this guy Ri-komo from here on."

What, we're naming it? Haruhiro thought, startled. *Ri-komo? Well, I don't care.*

Haruhiro and his group naturally lined up behind the Tokkis. Ranta was the only one trying to push in between Inui and Tada.

"Ri-komo, huh," Ranta said. "Hmm. You're right, he does look like a bat. He looks weak."

"I dunno. You can never tell, yeah?" Tokimune said, crouching down next to the ri-komo. "Hey, Ri-komo. Understand? You... are... Ri-komo. I... am... Tokimune. Okay?"

Ri-komo's eyes were wide, and its entire body shaking. It didn't look like it could understand what Tokimune was saying.

Tokimune shrugged. "You don't get it, huh? That figures. As for me, I don't really want to suddenly up and kill you for no good reason, or be hostile towards you. Hmm. What to do..."

"Abburoggurah," Ri-komo said—or something like that.

"Hmm?" Tokimune cocked his head to the side.

"Gurabburoadah."

"Yeah, no, I don't understand. I don't speak your language, either. What? Calm down. Talk slowly. Maybe we can communicate?"

"Aregoraburadeh, furaburaguraboradoh, zabaradiofuraburah."

"Man, I said to take it slowly—"

"Foah!"

Ri-komo suddenly tried to jump to its feet. But it couldn't do it. It never would.

Because of Tada. The glasses-wearing priest pulverized Ri-komo's head with a single blow of his warhammer.

"The guy was hopeless." Tada spun his warhammer around, resting it over his shoulder, then used the index finger of his left hand to adjust his now-bloodstained glasses. "Had to kill him. For now, they all die, all of them."

"Well, guess there's not much choice, huh?" Tokimune stood up. "It's kill-or-be-killed, and we can't do much about it now that you already killed him."

"They batbaric, yeah!" Anna-san said, hopping up and down. "Batbarians! No! You supposed to *laugh!* I make pun on bat and barbarian, yeah?!"

"Wah ha ha," Kikkawa gave an obviously fake laugh for Anna-san.

"Nice one, Anna-san! You're a laugh riot! A riot laugh! Gah ha ha ha ha!"

"Heh..." Inui adjusted his eyepatch. "Funny..."

"Really?" Mimorin was the only one who seemed doubtful. Though, that said, she was completely expressionless, and just tilted her head to the side a little.

"W-well, that settles that!" Ranta nodded. "Now what?! We kill anything that comes out! On the spot! Nice and simple! I like it! This is so my style!"

Haruhiro looked to Kuzaku, Shihoru, Yume, and Merry. Kuzaku was dumbfounded. Shihoru, Yume, and Merry were all taken aback.

Haruhiro gave a heavy sigh. "That was the right choice. Ri...Ri-komo..." *Yeah, I really don't like that name,* Haruhiro thought, but it would have felt stupid to propose an alternative. "...it seemed like it was going to attack. We don't know what we're dealing with, so to protect ourselves, it's safest to kill them, and I think that's the better choice."

"Man." Tada clicked his tongue with distaste. "Why've you gotta say stuff that's obvious?"

Uh oh...is he looking to pick a fight with me? Haruhiro wondered. *Could be. Not that I'm going to give him one.*

Haruhiro made a mental note that Tada was the fighting type. He'd had a vague sense before that he might be.

It was hard to come up with a response. If Haruhiro, the leader, was too humble, the party as a whole would get looked down on. Though, that said, he didn't want to clash with the guy.

Regardless, Haruhiro accepted Tada's glare. *I'm not gonna back down* was the one thing he had to show here.

Now, what was next? What would he do?

"It's a culture thing, you know." Tokimune interposed himself between Haruhiro and Tada, putting a hand on each of their shoulders. "We've got different cultures. Our party and Haruhiro's, that is. We've got to—what is it? Accept we have our differences? And have fun together? Yeah?"

"Oh, I have no problem with that," said Haruhiro.

Am I pushing back too hard? he wondered. *But Tada seems like the type to relentlessly mock anyone he looks down on. I feel like that's the kind of guy he is.*

"If we can have fun, I'll have fun," said Haruhiro. "But I think it's no good for us to force ourselves to hold back."

"Yeah, it's best not to force ourselves," Tada said, licking his lips. "It wouldn't last long, anyway. I can be very patient, though."

"Oh, can you?" Haruhiro said. "There's a surprise."

"Oh, yes, I can," said Tada. "You've got sleepy eyes, so maybe you're just not seeing me right."

Haruhiro took a deep breath. *That was close. I almost snapped there.*

"I was born with these eyes, and I can see just fine, Tada-san," he said.

"Oh, can you now?" Tada asked.

"Yes. What'll it be? Are we going to have fun?"

"Oh, I'm having fun," said Tada.

"Me, too," said Haruhiro. "Fancy that."

"Okay, Okay, Okay, Okay, Okayyyyyy!" Kikkawa grabbed both Haruhiro's and Tada's left hands and forced them to shake. "There you go, all made up! Happy, happy, smile, smile! We've gotta enjoy ourselves! Yeah! Harucchi, Tadacchi, both of you!"

Tada brushed Kikkawa's and Haruhiro's hands away, but he said no more.

Haruhiro quickly gave a short bow. "Sorry. For getting a little too cheeky there."

"Nah." Tada seemed to have been thrown off-balance by the apology, which was just what Haruhiro had been aiming for. "Well, it's fine."

Haruhiro figured this was about as good of a resolution as he could expect to get. He knew he wasn't the prideful sort, so apologizing and giving ground wasn't that painful for him. However, if it was going to be a disadvantage to the party for him to do so, that changed things.

Still, a high-handed attitude would only ruffle feathers. He needed to avoid conflict while also keeping up appearances. It was a pain in the butt, but he was the leader. He had to do it.

Haruhiro subtly covered his mouth with one hand and sighed. True, it was a pain, but he also felt a sense of accomplishment. That was another way he was plain and boring, and it irked him.

"Haruhiro!" a voice called.

"Yes? Bwuh—"

Wh-what? What just happened? Huh? Someone called my name? What is this? What is going on? I don't get it. There's a lot of people talking around me. Huh? What does it mean?

What? Huh? Breasts? Are these breasts? Breasts? Around my face? My face is buried in breasts? But they're not that soft, you know? Well, I'm not feeling them directly, I guess? There're clothes in between, I mean? Is that the problem? What problem? I don't know. I have no clue what's happening.

He was being hugged. By the giantess, Mimori. By Mimorin.

He was being hugged now. Tightly, so tightly. Mimorin was taller than Haruhiro. So Haruhiro's face ended up pressed against Mimori's breasts.

Mimorin put her arms around Haruhiro's back and squeezed him tight. It was kind of suffocating. Mimorin was rubbing her face up against his head. She gave off a sweet smell that didn't resemble anything he knew.

Yeah, I dunno what to make of this, he thought, dumbfounded. *That's it, you know. More than I thought, more than I imagined—it's like, what even is this? I expected them to be softer, squishier; to feel good, comfortable; for it to be a moving experience. I thought that's what it'd be like. But it's not. Apparently not.*

It hurts, and they aren't soft or anything. My dreams—they're shattered. I feel betrayed, somehow.

Like, what? That's all?

Like, I thought it'd be better than this! Come on, this isn't fair!

"There, there," Mimorin whispered to him.

Yeah, say that all you want, Haruhiro thought. *What is this?*

Seriously, what is this?

What is thiiiiiiiiiiiiiiiiiiiiiiiiiiiiiiis?!

"You did your best," said Mimorin.

"Huh?"

"There, there."

Despite himself.

Suddenly.

Unintentionally.

And without meaning to.

Without thinking, or knowing why—

—his eyes began to tear up.

No, no, no, no, no, no, no, no, no, no, no, no, no, no, no, no, noooooo! he screamed silently. *What good is crying going to do? And, wait, what is this? It's too sudden. What? What do you know? You couldn't know anything. If someone who doesn't know my circumstances says that to me, I'm just gonna be confused, and maybe a little angry, too. What is with you? Who do you think you are? You frighten me. Seriously. You're scary. Sorry to say it, but you're huge. Way too damn huge. Not that I'd actually say that.*

"Um, er, Mimorin-san..." he mumbled.

"No. You don't need the -san," she said. "Mimorin."

"...Mimorin."

"What?"

"Could you get away from me...?" he ventured.

"Okay." Mimorin backed away surprisingly easily.

Well, good, thought Haruhiro. If she'd refused, he'd have had an even bigger problem.

"Mimorin..." Tokimune mumbled, sounding uncharacteristically dumbfounded. "Mimorin, huh. I see. So that's how it is. Haruhiro, huh. I just don't get Mimori..."

"Mimori's sure got awful taste," Tada said, snorting derisively.

"Heh..." Inui had a look on his face like he'd just bitten into something unpleasant. "So, this is fate, is it?"

What's supposed to be fate? Haruhiro backed away.

Mimorin was looking down at him, her expression as blank as ever. She had no expression, but he could feel a passion in her gaze.

"Whew." Anna-san shook her head left and right. "Anna-san not really get it either, yeah. *However,* Mimorin, she loves bizarre and low-quality things, yeah?"

"Bizarre and low-quality..." Ranta burst out laughing. "Wah ha ha ha ha! Yeah, Parupiro, quaint, that's you, all right! I see, I see, bizarre and low-quality, huh! That's why! I can accept that! Gwah ha ha ha ha ha! Congrats, you bizarre and low-quality thing!"

"...Ehe... Ranta... You don't even pass for low-quality... You're lower than low-quality... Ehehehe..."

"Oh, be quiet!" Ranta hollered. "Shut up, Zodiac-kun! You're gonna make me cry, dammit!"

"Uh, well," Shihoru started hesitantly. "Haruhiro-kun, congrat... ulations?"

"No, it's not..." Haruhiro stopped. His mind went blank; he couldn't find the words.

"Hooooh," Yume's eyes went wide. "Yume doesn't really get it, but it feels like somethin' to be celebratin.'"

"Congratulations," Merry said, in a deadpan tone for some reason.

"Grats," Kuzaku said, suddenly bowing his head.

"No, hold on, wai—i-i-isn't this weird?! It's weird, right?! I mean, I don't feel anything—M-Mimori-san doesn't either."

"Mimorin," Mimori corrected him calmly.

"Mimorin doesn't really feel that way...either... You don't, right? Um... What is it? Erm, you were consoling me? Encouraging me? Something like that? Out of that sort of...human love and compassion? Was it...that sort of thing...? It was...right?"

"Love!" Ranta writhed with laughter. "Love! It's love now! Loveeeeee! We've got love here! L! O! V! E! Loveeeeeeeeeee...!"

"You, just go die already!" Haruhiro spouted off. He knew it wasn't a thing he should say, even in jest, but he didn't feel all that bad for having said it.

Haruhiro turned to face Mimorin. He didn't have the courage to look her in the eye. It was too scary to look into her eyes right now. "That's how it is...right? It is, yeah? Um...s-sympathy? Maybe? Or pity? That sort of thing..."

"I want to raise you," Mimorin said, plain as day.

To raise me? Like, lift me up, or something? No, that's not it. Then what is it?

"...Huh?" Haruhiro said.

"You're cute. So, I want to raise you."

"Raise me—do you mean...like, as a pet...?"

"Yes. I want to raise you as a pet."

Haruhiro stared at her. "I-I can't be your pet, you know? I mean, I'm human..."

"Too bad," she said regretfully.

"Well, that's that," he said with relief.

"But I won't give up," Mimori said forcefully. Then she sniffled.

She's kinda—wait, are her eyes tearing up? I think so.

"Someday, I'll make you my pet," she said.

"Oh, will you?" That was all Haruhiro could answer.

What is this? he thought, dumbfounded.

6. Welcome to the Realm of Dusk

Twelfth, thirteenth, fourteenth, fifteenth...

The searching of rooms continued.

As they went deeper and deeper, the eggs really were getting larger, if only a little at a time. Comparing one room's eggs with the next, the difference was more or less unnoticeable, but comparing the first room to the sixteenth, there was a great difference in the eggs' sizes. While they might not have doubled, they were at least half again as big.

They hadn't met another ri-komo since the first one.

What was that ri-komo? What was it doing before we found it? Were these ri-komo eggs? Or not? Haruhiro didn't know.

The seventeenth room was big. Or maybe it just felt that way.

"There are...no eggs," Haruhiro said slowly.

Without anything casting light, it was pitch black. There was no way to tell if there were any ri-komos.

He didn't sense any presences there, but Haruhiro thoroughly searched the room with a lantern just to be sure.

There were no ri-komos.

There was, however, a hole in the corner. Not in the wall. It was a round hole in the ground, about 1.2 meters in diameter. A vertical hole.

They all surrounded the hole.

Haruhiro crouched down and thrust the hand he was holding the lantern with into the hole.

"The bottom is...not visible, at all. It goes down quite a ways, though."

"Hmm." Mimorin nodded, tucking her chin in. "Let's search."

For some reason, Mimorin was crouching at Haruhiro's side. Well, that reason was clear—it was because she wanted to raise him like a pet. However, even crouching, she was a gigantic woman. Just huge.

"You could use those as, like, hand-and-footholds, don't you think? Over there." Kikkawa motioned towards the surface of the hole's sides with his chin. "Even without a ladder, you could, like, get up and down. Don't you think?"

It was true; there were protrusions it looked like they could grab with their hands or hook their feet on. It might not be quick, but if they put their minds to it, they could go down.

"Zodiac-kun." Ranta turned to the demon. "You go down first for us."

"...Kehe... Ranta... I wouldn't mind pushing you down it... Kehehehe..."

A flat refusal.

"Heh..." Inui flipped a coin and caught it in the palm of his hand. "Let's try with this..."

"*Ouch!*" Anna-san cried out. "That what Anna-san was thinking of doing, yeah?!"

"Too late... Heh..." Inui sent the coin down the hole.

They listened for it.

Soon, there was a clinking sound. It seemed the hole had a bottom, at least. It could only be so deep.

"Well..." Haruhiro sighed slightly. "I'll go in."

"Sorry about this, thief." Tokimune flashed his white teeth in a smile.

"Do your best," Mimorin said impassively.

It'd be awkward to just straight-up ignore her. Haruhiro tied the lantern around his waist, the corner of his lips twitching slightly as he nodded. Feeling bothered, not very happy, put upon, and carrying all sorts of other unsatisfying feelings, he went into the hole. Or down the hole, rather. Hooking his hands and feet on the bumps, he descended.

Partway down, he started to wonder, *Is it really smart for the leader to be scouting ahead? It's something I always do, but the leader has the important role of making decisions for the party as a whole. If they lost their leader, no matter how plain and mediocre of a leader I am, that would end badly. Scouting carries a fair number of risks. It can lead to serious injury or, well, death, so maybe it's not something the leader should be doing...?*

It was something that'd just occurred to him. Right now, they had Tokimune, so things would work out even if something were, theoretically, to happen to Haruhiro. There was the issue of if he could leave it to any of his other comrades, too. While Ranta and Yume were both quick, owing to their jobs, neither of them had the personality for it. They lacked the ability to concentrate.

Who did it for the Tokkis? Maybe Inui, since he used to be a thief, too?

Though, this was the Tokkis he was thinking about, after all. They might not bother with a little thing like scouting and just, *wham,* charge in and go *bam* and *boom* and be done with it.

No, it wasn't that scouting was a little thing. He didn't hate doing it. These sorts of jobs that were pretty plain, but that someone had to do—that had a real effect on the outcome if done right, but didn't earn much praise, yet still came with a sense of self-satisfaction—they were the jobs Haruhiro secretly enjoyed.

I must say, I'm not a clever person, he thought. *But that's okay, I'm fine like this.* Even if he tried to force himself to change, he'd soon be unmasked for what he really was.

In a plain, ordinary way, without making any noise, he went down the hole.

He reached the bottom. There was a path. He couldn't see what was down it, but he didn't sense anything nearby.

"It looks clear," Haruhiro called up. "We can keep going. Come down."

Tokimune and then each of the others in turn came down. At times like this, Haruhiro thought it might've been best if Tokimune had stayed up until everyone else was down, but he opted not to say anything.

The path narrowed from here on. It was around two meters high, less than a meter and a half across. It wasn't impossible to walk two abreast, but it would've been cramped, so Haruhiro took point, with Tokimune behind him to the left, Kikkawa diagonally to the right behind Tokimune, and so on. They advanced in an unorthodox zigzag column, or one and a half columns.

It wasn't just Haruhiro and his group being quiet now; the Tokkis were, too.

Something's probably going to happen here. There's got to be something. Haruhiro felt his pulse racing. *No, calm down,* he told himself. *Level head. Keep a level head. If I get too nervous, that narrows my range of vision and my body tenses up.*

The path was more or less flat and straight. At some point, Haruhiro noticed he'd started going awfully slowly. It might be okay to pick up the pace a bit.

"Just now..." Haruhiro stopped walking and turned around. "Did someone say something?"

"Hmm?" Tokimune shrugged his shoulders. "Could be. Did anyone say anything?"

No one raised their hand. Everyone shook their head.

"Did you hear something?" Tokimune asked him.

"No. Well, I thought I did...maybe? That's as far as it went. Oh..." Haruhiro brought his index finger to his lips. Everyone held their breath.

I can hear them, he thought.

"...Aruburuburah."

"...Furaguraburubaradirah."

"...Shurubiraburaharagureroh."

"...Pyuraryugadih."

"...Aburaguh."

Those were the sorts of voices he heard.

"Ri-komos..." Kikkawa said in a small voice. "...You think, like, there're a lot of them?"

Haruhiro took a deep breath, laying the lantern down on the

ground. "I'll go take a look."

"You going to be okay?" It was unusual for Tokimune to sound worried for him like this.

That's a bad omen, Haruhiro thought nervously. *No, no.*

"If you want, I can go with you, you know?" Ranta said, sounding all self-important.

"If my only other alternative was to go with you, I'd be eight hundred million times better by myself, so no thanks," Haruhiro said.

"You're so not cute. Augh!" Ranta was cowering. Someone had whacked him with their staff.

"Haruhiro is cute." It was Mimorin, expressionless as ever.

"How so?" Shihoru asked.

She had probably just asked the question because it'd popped into her head, but it was still a little mean.

No, maybe not.

No. No it wasn't. Haruhiro wasn't cute at all. He didn't want anyone thinking he was cute.

"The way he's pitiful, but he still puts in all this meaningless effort," Mimorin responded.

I see. Haruhiro pinched the bridge of his nose. *I see.*

It was true, he was pitiful, and he might have been trying too hard in spite of that. In fact, he was shocked she had hit so close to the mark, and he wasn't sure he could recover from it. Well, even if he was fine with that—which he wasn't—how was that supposed to be cute?

"Mimoriiiin..." Anna-san said as she hugged Mimorin around the waist, which was pretty high up for her with how short she was. "Now I sort of get it, yeah."

"Right?" Mimorin nodded.

"That *bad*... Anna-san think it is...enduring. No... Endearing? Subset, type, of pity? Yeah? He is pathetic? Right?" Anna-san asked.

Mimorin cocked her head to the side and thought for a moment, but ultimately didn't answer Anna-san's question before turning back to Haruhiro. "Haruhiro, you're cute."

"Uh... Thanks," he said.

"I want to keep you as a pet. Let me."

"I can't."

"Really?"

"Yeah."

"Don't die."

"Okay."

Haruhiro headed out as if trying to escape.

Scouting. I have to scout. I'll give scouting my all. I'm going to do the most perfect scouting job ever. I'll scout like no one else. I am going to scout. Now, I am going to be the scouting master. I am the best scout ever. I want to be able to puff up my chest and say that with pride. Okay, no, not really, but right now, it's time to scout. For now, I'm gonna scout.

Use Sneaking. Ahh, this sure is fun, Sneaking. I love it. Sneaking. I'm pathetic, but I'll work my butt off for no good reason. What's wrong with working hard?! Nothing. I'm already pitiful, so if I don't at least try hard, I'll be way too pitiful, you know? I'll be like Anna-san. Sigh...

Focus. Gotta focus.

The path went on without winding. He kept hearing the ri-komos talking. He didn't really understand, but maybe they were shooting the breeze? It didn't have a particularly urgent tone. As he felt his way forward, the voices grew louder, so the one thing he could be sure of was that there were ri-komos up ahead. *It was the right decision to leave the lantern behind*—he thought. Probably.

He could see light up ahead. A slight, weak light. He approached it.

Just before coming out into a wider area, Haruhiro stopped.

"Aburerah, burareryoh, samuragerasshuh."

"Bagashoburirah, faiabushuh, fakkashuburyoh."

"Rabureshuburaruroh, fanafarabushoh, ireburesshoruttoh."

They're there. There. They're coming now. From over there.

The room's got considerable height, width, and depth. But, what exactly is it like inside? And what's this faint light? He squinted his eyes. No good. Can't see.

Haruhiro turned his neck, then his shoulders. Nodding, he poked his head out a little.

It's big—though, that said, it's not ridiculously wide. Well, maybe ten meters across. Thereabouts. I dunno how high the roof is, or how far back it goes. There're light sources all over. There're lots of holes, big and small, in the rock wall, and it looks like there's a blue light coming out of them. Seems like the ri-komos are inside those holes. Where the holes are—hanging upside down? There're ri-komos there, too. And the ri-komos, they're talking about something? Looks like.

Is it a ri-komo nest?

That's probably what this place is.

Haruhiro turned back before the ri-komos could find him. Haruhiro was welcomed back by a silent group of eleven volunteer soldiers and one Zodiac-kun.

"Looks like a ri-komo nest," Haruhiro said. "There're a ton of them. More than ten or twenty. Charging in is, well, not something I'd want to do. Personally speaking."

"Hmm…" Tokimune had a pensive look on his face.

"Leave this one to me," Tada said, the lantern's light flashing off his glasses as he spoke. "The way I see it, the ri-komos won't attack. I'll go and check that now. You guys, at least get ready to run in case you have to."

"Hold up," Ranta said, a not-so-daring smile that was really a mix of fear and bravado on his face. "We can't have the Tokkis do everything for us. Let me come, too."

"…Kehe… Give it up…Ranta… Kehehe… You can try to act cool, but you never will be…"

"That's not true! I was damn cool just now, wasn't I?!" Ranta shouted. "It was on the level where you might fall for me in spite of yourselves, right? Right? Come on? Right?"

Ranta looked to the girls. He received no response but cold stares.

"No, um…" Haruhiro scratched his head. "It's clearly dangerous, so maybe you should give up?"

"No." Tada adjusted his glasses with his left index finger. "Absolutely not. Listen, Tokimune. If things go south, run away without me."

"Sure," Tokimune said. "Okay, let's do that."

"He accepted that easily…" Kuzaku mumbled.

"You're okay with that, yeah, Haruhiro?" Tokimune asked. The fact that Tokimune had checked with him actually came as a bit of a surprise. "Okay, get going, Tada."

Well, I still hadn't given you a response yet, though, Haruhiro thought.

Tada shouldered his warhammer, humming as he walked off at a leisurely pace.

"W-wait, wait! Me too! Me too!" Ranta and Zodiac-kun chased

after him.

"Wow..." Yume looked on, dumbfounded.

Merry cleared her throat. She might have been trying to calm herself.

Haruhiro sighed. He seemed to punctuate nearly everything with a sigh. Sighs were the one thing he could believe in. No, it wasn't a question of believing or not believing. Just...

"I'm going to be following a bit behind Tada-san," he said. "Tokimune-san, just in case, have everyone ready to run away."

"Okay." Tokimune nodded. "Thanks for your hard work."

"Haruhiro." Mimorin nodded to him expressionlessly. "Live."

"Okay."

He was happy she was rooting for him, at least. No, maybe not so much.

Haruhiro stayed three meters behind Ranta and Zodiac-kun.

Tada was still humming to himself. The guy was having way too much fun. He had to be off in the head.

The most normal-looking one wasn't just crazy, he was the craziest. That was the pattern their group had ended up following.

Tada looked like he was headed off on a merry stroll, but Haruhiro was on edge. Ranta was walking funny, too. He was totally spooked. Compared to Tada, Ranta's behavior was almost cute.

This was a new thought for Haruhiro. Ranta being cute.

Tada didn't stop once, or slow, before he entered the nest. Ranta was hesitant, but Zodiac-kun pushed him from behind.

"Whoa... Hey! Zodiac-kun?! Stop?! I need to be mentally prepared before I do this, you know?!"

"...Kehe... Shut up and *die*..."

"I'm not gonna dieeeeeeee...!"

"Ranta," Haruhiro warned him, even though it was already too late, "you're too loud, man."

"Whoa?!" Ranta jumped.

"Ha ha!" Tada turned back to them and gave his warhammer a swing. "Don't sweat it! It's no problem! If I'm on the mark, the ri-komos won't come and attack us!"

The ri-komo voices...had stopped.

It was silent.

"See?" Tada said boastfully, looking around the nest. "Just like I thought. These guys are really cowardly. They're not exactly belligerent."

"No, but, Tada-san, you killed one of them in the other room," said Haruhiro.

"That's when I figured it out," he said confidently. "From the feeling when I hit him? I knew the guy was weak."

"So, it's that sort of... How should I say it...? Instinctual thing, huh?" Haruhiro asked.

"Life, man," said Tada. "It's not about reason."

"Ohh!" Ranta fell to one knee, clutching his chest. "A great line is *born!* You're right! 'Life's not about reason,' is it?! Tada-san, you're awesome!"

"Don't praise me so much." Tada hit his warhammer on his shoulder as he adjusted his glasses. "I'll catch your stupidity!"

"Wah ha ha! No, no, noooo! There you go, being like that again, Tada-saaaan!"

What's with these two? thought Haruhiro. *Ranta's always been an idiot, but maybe Tada's an idiot, too? Are they both idiots?*

The ri-komos remained silent, showing no sign of moving. Though, that said, this could be the calm before a storm, maybe? Haruhiro, honestly, didn't feel safe at all.

"Haruhiro, you come, too," Tada beckoned to him.

"...I think I'd rather not."

"Just get over here," Tada said.

"Yeah, Parupiroooo," Ranta yelled. "Don't chicken out on us, you idiot!"

"Hurry up," Tada said. "Or I'm gonna slug you."

"If you hit me with that thing, I could easily die, you know..." Haruhiro muttered.

He probably wasn't serious. But, this being Tada, Haruhiro couldn't be sure, so he was left with no choice but to comply.

Haruhiro hesitantly walked into the nest. It was true, the ri-komo they'd met in the earlier room hadn't been that tough. Still, if the ri-komos swarmed them en masse, they would be a threat. Or rather, the difference in numbers was so great, Haruhiro and the other two might be mincemeat in no time. He could feel death so very near. Mimorin had told him to live, but that might not be possible.

Or maybe it would be.

The ri-komos hadn't moved, after all. Their voices were silent.

"Ranta." Tada gestured towards the path they came from with his chin. "Go call Tokimune. Haruhiro and I will wait here."

"Yes, sir!" Ranta yelled.

"...Kehehe... You're like a gopher, Ranta... Kehe... It suits you... Kehehehe..."

"Shut up! It's fine! Tada's the man with the quote of the day!" Ranta made that nonsensical declaration and then ran off down the path. Zodiac-kun followed him.

Now Haruhiro was alone with Tada. No... there were a ton of rikomos surrounding them. It was hard to call that being alone together.

"Haruhiro."

"What?"

Tada didn't say anything more right away. A moment passed before he said, "Take good care of Mimori for me."

"Say what?"

"She's bigger than I am, and her taste is awful, and I never know what she's thinking, and she won't let me call her Mimorin, and she pisses me off, but we're still comrades," Tada said.

"No... I'm not the guy to ask," Haruhiro said.

"You're not satisfied?"

"Huh? No, I don't think that's the problem here..."

"Her boobs are *huge,* man," said Tada. "Though, she's huge in general."

"I don't think that comes into it," said Haruhiro.

"It does," Tada said with certainty. "Man, you make fun of boobs; you'll be crying for them later."

"Is that how it works?"

"What? You've never cried for boobs before?" Tada asked.

"...Never."

"I have."

"Huh."

"You're not going to ask?" Tada asked. "You're not gonna ask for all the details?"

"Do you want to talk about it?" Haruhiro asked.

"Like *hell* I would," Tada snapped. "It's my own private business. You must be off in the head, man."

You're the last guy I want to hear that from. Haruhiro looked around the area. The ri-komos were staying quiet.

"Don't tell me... you got us alone together just so you could say that?" Haruhiro asked.

"Yeah," said Tada. "Don't say I did it 'just' for that. It's a big deal, got it?"

"I don't have any special feelings for her, so that's that," said Haruhiro.

"You're very clear on that, huh? You're an honest guy. When you're so good-natured, how are you so screwed in the head? What's *wrong* with you?"

"What's wrong, indeed," Haruhiro said. *With you, that is.*

Soon, Ranta came back with Tokimune and the others. Ranta, Zodiac-kun, and the Tokkis came into the nest like it was no big deal, but Kuzaku, Shihoru, Yume, and Merry were timid.

That's normal, Haruhiro thought. *It's soothing to see. Normal is good. Normal is best.*

"Ohh." Tokimune shaded his eyes with one hand and looked around restlessly. "This is the ri-komo nest, huh? Hmm. There're a whole lot of them."

The ri-komos that'd been keeping quiet until just a little while ago were now making a lot of noise. Haruhiro was beside himself with worry.

"Wh...what do we do? From here on?" he stammered.

"We go on, that's what," said Tokimune.

"...That figures," Haruhiro muttered.

"You want to go back? Then do it. We're staying. Actually, we're gonna go even further, you know?"

Tokimune was saying that they didn't need Haruhiro to move forward with their exploration. If Haruhiro wanted to pull out, the Tokkis would continue exploring alone.

"Let's go," Haruhiro said.

"Wouldn't have it any other way," Tokimune said, flashing his white teeth.

I can't help but feel I got egged into that one, Haruhiro thought, frustrated. *Everything's moving at the Tokkis' pace. But if I fight with them for control, I can't see any way I come out on top. Do I just have to go with the flow?*

If the ri-komos decided to remove the intruders, Haruhiro and the others—in that instant, it'd be over. It was hard to predict any result but their utter annihilation.

Taking the lantern from Kuzaku and advancing in two columns, Haruhiro wondered if these people understood that. It couldn't be that they had no concept of the danger. They were taking a calculated risk. That was probably perfectly natural for the Tokkis.

So, these are the kinds of people... Haruhiro thought.

These were the kinds of people suited to the volunteer soldier life. Not plain, boring people like Haruhiro, but people like the Tokkis, or, well, like Ranta, who were a little off in the head.

Haruhiro was doing something he was ill-suited to. Was there meaning in doing what he could, ill-suited or not? Or were there things he could do precisely because he was ill-suited to the task?

The ri-komos' screeching showed no sign of abating—but they took no other action.

"If it were just these guys," Tokimune craned his neck as he spoke, "they'd be crushed in no time. The Wonder Hole is not a forgiving place."

Haruhiro more or less got what he was saying. The Wonder Hole was a place for survival of the fittest, where the strong ate the weak. Creatures that couldn't defend their territory would quickly be exterminated.

Even the three demi-humans, seen as the weakest races in the Wonder Hole, could be quite fierce, depending on their enemies. The ri-komos, though this was only based on Haruhiro's current impressions, were too passive, and too weak.

The path stretched on straight ahead. There were openings to turn left, right, and right, in that order, but Tokimune ignored them and went straight. Then they came to a T-junction.

The ri-komos made a racket, but they didn't attack.

Haruhiro and the others turned left.

There were two openings to turn left. When they passed them by, they stopped seeing that dim glow. They no longer heard the ri-komos' voices.

"Is this the end of the nest?" Haruhiro murmured.

Tokimune pointed up ahead. "Nah, there's a path. And besides—"

"Yeah."

I know, Haruhiro thought. *The wind.*

There was a flow of air coming from up ahead. It was fair to call it wind.

Haruhiro hadn't been relaxing, but he was suddenly tensing himself for something. He didn't know what the reason was. Haruhiro didn't have a clear basis for why, but Haruhiro's expectations for what was to come were building. For whatever reason, everyone else seemed the same.

The path started to snake. That, and it developed a slight slope. Upward.

"Huh?" Ranta raised his voice, looking left and right and behind them. "Zodiac-kun's gone..."

"Didn't you just run out of time?" Yume asked.

"That can't be it. Hmm..." Ranta cocked his head to the side. "Well, it's fine."

It's fine? Haruhiro thought for a moment. *Well, I guess it's fine,* he reconsidered, sensing that he might be a little hasty. *I want to get to the end of this path as soon as I can. I feel like something will be there. No, there definitely will be something there.*

The wind is cold.

There's light up ahead.

That light is—

"Heh..." Inui growled, low. "We're outside, you say?"

Outside, Haruhiro thought. *No, that's absurd. I mean, we're pretty far down. This is underground. We can't be outside. But...that light is almost like we're outside. Then there's this wind.*

"Ohhhhhhh! I can't wait!" Ranta rushed forward.

"You...!" Tada chased after him.

"Ha ha ha ha ha ha ha ha!" Tokimune started running as he laughed.

"No fair! Me too, me too, me too!" Kikkawa yelled, following after them.

"Heh..." Inui went, as well.

"*Hah!* There is no cure for fool!" Anna-san yelled something insulting and chased after them at a sprint. "Then, I go, too, you know! I must go, yeah!"

Mimorin was expressionless, silent, and walked forward with

great strides.

Haruhiro looked to Kuzaku, Shihoru, Yume, and Merry before chasing after them at a jog. He understood some of what Ranta and the others were feeling, even if he didn't want to.

After all, what if this really *was* outside?

He didn't think that it was, of course. That was impossible.

But...what about the one-in-a-million chance it was? That'd be something of an event. No, it might be more than just "something of" an event. At the very least, for pitiful Haruhiro, the mediocre guy who tried too hard, it would be a major event.

Even though he wasn't running full tilt, he was getting short of breath.

Outside, he thought. *Ahh.*

"Wow!" Haruhiro cried.

The sky. He could see something like the sky.

"Hyohhhhhhhhhhhhhhhhhhhhhhh!" Ranta let out a bizarre cry of sheer amazement.

"This is it!" Tokimune cried, having apparently gotten ahead of Tada.

"Ha ha!" Tada laughed.

"Schwing!" Kikkawa wasn't making any sense.

What's 'schwing' even supposed to mean?

"Heh... Ha ha ha ha ha!" Inui gave a loud villain laugh.

"Oh my God! Oh my God!" Anna-san was going crazy.

Mimorin had stopped and stood still right after she got outside. The wind was bracing. Strong enough to make Mimorin's thick hair stream in the breeze.

Haruhiro stopped next to Mimorin. "*This...*"

Encountering a scene like this, and only being able to say *"This..."* was an accurate manifestation of Haruhiro's mediocrity, and it hurt.

"Fwahhhhhhh..." Yume had her mouth open wide.

"I can't believe it," Shihoru whispered as she held her hat down.

"Seriously?" Kuzaku narrowed his eyes.

"This is—" Merry shook her head back and forth, beginning to reach out towards Kuzaku before she pulled her hand back.

There was a sky.

Haruhiro and the others were below a sky studded with deep blue, blue with a light red undertone, purple, orange, yellow, red, and all the colors in between.

It was the evening sky.

Behind them was a hole that just opened into the side of a hill, and the sky spread out in all directions. They saw the sky at twilight nearly every day, but this was different. The hues were too vibrant. No, that wasn't all. The sun rose in the east and set in the west. When the sun went down, it was the western sky that was red. When the sun rose, it was the opposite. But not in this sky.

He couldn't tell the cardinal directions, but it was red all over, with yellow as well.

There was no sign of any sun.

It was almost as if the sky had been splattered with different-colored paints.

Ranta and all of the Tokkis, except Mimorin, were rushing down the grass-covered slope. There were whitish pillar-like rocks dotted around the hill.

Haruhiro noticed that Tokimune, the others, and the pillars cast no shadow. Of course, it was the same with Haruhiro.

"No," Mimorin mumbled. "This isn't our world."

"Yeah," Haruhiro nodded. "It's another world."

Grimgar of Fantasy and Ash

7. An Issue of Time

The Dusk Realm. That was the name Anna-san gave it.

"It" being the other world that spread out beyond the ri-komo nest, of course.

Haruhiro thought it wasn't a bad name, honestly, and that maybe they should have her come up with a better name for the ri-komos, too.

Their first day of exploration after discovering the Dusk Realm ended with them just wandering around in circles on that initial hill. The next day they planned to bring food, water, and tents so that they could continue their exploration without going home every day. If they could find a good spot, they wanted to set up a base camp for their expedition. For that, they were hoping to at least find a water source.

There were many things they needed to think about, and all of them were fun.

That night, Haruhiro couldn't get a wink of sleep. He also didn't feel like going to his usual place and drinking. He needed to get some sleep so that he was properly rested for tomorrow.

Time to sleep. I've got to sleep. I'm gonna sleep.

The more he thought that, the less able to sleep he was. He started to find Ranta's snoring even more irritating than usual, he got pissed off, and—somehow, he still managed to fall asleep eventually, then woke up.

They got ready, then headed out for their meeting place with the Tokkis, the hole just past the kingdom of devils.

Haruhiro didn't have a mechanical timepiece because they were expensive, so he didn't know the precise time, but they left the Lonesome Field Outpost at around 7:00. The Wonder Hole was about a kilometer northwest of the outpost. Even considering the time it would take to pass through the valley of holes, the muryan nest, and the kingdom of devils, they'd probably make it in time for the agreed meetup at 9:00.

They didn't encounter an ustrel, so they presumably arrived well before 9:00. Then they waited for what was easily an hour.

"...They're late!" Ranta stomped his feet indignantly. "We've been waiting for, like, half a day, you know?! The sun's gonna set!"

"We haven't been waitin' that long," Yume looked half-exasperated, half-exhausted. "But, still. They sure are late. Yesterday, they were here on time."

"Do you think something happened?" Shihoru frowned and let out a little sigh.

"Before we could meet up, you mean?" Merry looked at her left wrist. Tired of waiting or not, this was the Wonder Hole. She couldn't let Protection wear off.

"Ahh..." Kuzaku had been squatting for a while now. "Maybe they came a bit late, then ran into an ustrel...or something?"

"Would an ustrel actually give them trouble?" Haruhiro crossed his arms. "I wonder."

"What do you say we just go on ahead?" Ranta snickered to himself evilly.

"That'd be like we were tryin' to get ahead of a start on them." Yume puffed up her cheeks.

"You mean a head start..." Haruhiro corrected her, then twisted his neck. "...Ah."

"They wouldn't have." Shihoru was quick on the uptake. Or perhaps those who this idea would and wouldn't occur to might have more to do with their individual personalities.

"Hm?" Ranta blinked, looking back and forth from Haruhiro to Shihoru.

He's an idiot, and half-asses everything, but he's not sly and underhanded, Haruhiro thought.

"Huh?" Merry seemed to have realized. "...They couldn't have."

"So, basically..." Kuzaku looked to the hole. "...It's not that they haven't come yet. They've already gone on ahead."

"Well, it's not like we know that for sure, you know...?" Haruhiro said.

I don't think we do. They wouldn't do that. That was what Haruhiro wanted to think. *But...I can't rule it out.*

"Well, it *is* the Tokkis, after all..." he said slowly.

They had an unpredictable side to them. The idea might pop into their heads, and they'd go, *Are we gonna do this? Are we?* and then just go ahead and do it. What's more, they wouldn't feel bad about it in the least.

"Either way, don't you think we should go?" Ranta said with uncharacteristic seriousness. "If they're late, it's their own fault. If they're trying to steal a march on us, then it's even more their fault. We've already wasted enough time. Time is money, they say. There's no reason for us to stay put here any longer."

That all sounded reasonable. Despite having come out of Ranta's mouth.

"Why don't we go?" Kuzaku stood up. "I'm tired of waiting."

There were no objections, so onward they went.

First, they passed through the round tunnel, then the seventeen egg rooms, which they could've ignored, but just to be safe, they gave them a cursory inspection. They didn't see a single ri-komo.

They headed down the vertical hole into the ri-komo nest.

There are too many nests in the Wonder Hole, Haruhiro thought. *We should have given the area a different name.*

A ways before they reached the ri-komo nest, Haruhiro noticed something had changed. It was strangely loud. The ri-komos had been talking about something yesterday, too, but this time, they seemed far more noisy than they had been before.

"Yeah, something's weird." Ranta cast the spell to summon Zodiac-kun.

"...Eh heh... Eh heh heh... Finally... Today Ranta dies... Eh heh heh heh... Eh heh..."

"You never change, huh, Zodiac-kun..." said Haruhiro.

This was no time to be impressed with the demon. Haruhiro was being pressed to make a decision. But, well, that was nothing new.

"I'll go take a look," he decided. "Everyone else, stay here. If it's dangerous, I'll shout, so run away immediately."

"Got it." Ranta put a hand on Haruhiro's shoulder, sticking his tongue out of the corner of his mouth and winking. "If it comes down to it, we'll abandon you and run. Don't you worry about that."

While, yes, Haruhiro had meant for them to do just that, it still pissed him off. But, he knew his anger would only make Ranta happy.

Haruhiro left the lantern behind and used Sneaking to scout ahead. Stopping just in front of the ri-komo nest, he tried to get a feel for the situation.

Yeah, they really are excited about something, was his impression. Was there some cause? Or was it common for the ri-komos to make this much of a ruckus?

They're just noisy, that's all, Haruhiro thought to himself, working up his courage, then deciding to try going a little ways into the nest.

All right! He went in.

Nothing changed. Nothing happened. The ri-komos were scattered all over, the same as before.

Maybe there was something that Haruhiro just didn't notice. And wait—there was something coming his way from over on the other side.

A ri-komo? he thought. *Apparently not. It looks human...* Or so he thought, but when it came time to make a call on what to do, Haruhiro wasn't sure.

A person? Who...?

There were only twelve people who knew this place existed, Haruhiro included. If he thought about it normally, it would have to be one of them. In other words, one of the Tokkis. But that was...

One single person, Haruhiro thought. *Just one person.*

They're still far off, and it's not that bright here, so I can't see very well.

All I can say for sure is that they look human-like. They might not be human. They could be some other human-looking creature. A dangerous one, maybe. And possibly the reason the ri-komos are making so much noise.

"No..." Haruhiro shook his head.

That's a human. He's walking this way. Or rather, it's like he's trying to run, but can't. He's dragging his leg behind him. Is he injured?

He's stopped. Looks like he's resting for a moment.

Haruhiro began to walk. After a moment, he recognized...

"Kikkawa?!"

"...Harucchi," the man said.

I got a reply. Looks like I was right. Kikkawa. It's Kikkawa.

Haruhiro rushed over to Kikkawa. He wasn't sounding cheerful enough. Haruhiro knew it was Kikkawa, but he didn't know how bad his injuries were.

"What's up? Why are you here? What happened?" Haruhiro burst out.

"...Sorry." Kikkawa sat down. "Sorry, Harucchi. Like, seriously, I apologize. But, I..."

"Don't worry about that," said Haruhiro. "No apologies for now. It can wait. Can you stand?"

"...Yeah. Somehow."

"Okay," said Haruhiro. "We'll head back to where the others are for now. You're hurt, right?"

"It's nothing major," said Kikkawa. "In my case..."

"We'll need to have Merry fix you up." Haruhiro lent Kikkawa his shoulder.

"It's nothing major. In my case..."

The way he'd said that bothered Haruhiro.

On the way back, Haruhiro tried asking, "Where are Tokimune-san and the others?"

"...In the Dusk Realm," managed Kikkawa. "All of us went. We set out this morning, while it was still dark out. We were trying to get ahead of you. Sorry, Harucchi..."

"Like I said, don't worry about that," said Haruhiro. "So? Why are you alone back here?"

"They told me to go. So here I am."

"I can't tell what happened from just that," said Haruhiro. "Did Tokimune-san tell you to run away?"

"Yeah... That guy, like, says I'm the Tokkis' lucky charm. That's why, like, he sent me back to the Wonder Hole alone...to call for help. He figured you guys'd be at the meet-up point."

"Help?" Haruhiro went pale. He hadn't even imagined a situation like this. It was bad. Really bad. "...Any losses?"

"They're alive," Kikkawa said.

Haruhiro let out a sigh of relief.

"...But only as far as I know."

"That figures," Haruhiro said, nodding. "Some time must have passed... Well, even so, it means there's some hope for them."

"Hope, huh..." Kikkawa sniffled.

"Dammit," Haruhiro muttered. "Why did this have to happen?"

Haruhiro brought Kikkawa back to where Ranta and the others were and had Merry treat him. Kikkawa had wounds on his left leg, right shoulder, and a deep one in his belly. He'd been in a pretty dangerous state.

"They do something underhanded like try to steal a march on us, and then this happens to them! Pathetic!" Ranta punched his right fist into the palm of his left hand.

"Still, that doesn't mean we can abandon them..." Haruhiro said.

"First, we need to get a precise account of what happened," said Shihoru. She was right.

"Right..." While Kikkawa had finished being healed, he'd still bled out a lot. He might've been feeling woozy, because he stayed sitting on the ground as he talked. "It was just... Remember yesterday? There was nothing dangerous then, so, honestly, we may have let our guards down a little..."

"Mm-hm," Yume crouched down next to Kikkawa, patting him on the head to console him. "There wasn't anythin' dangerous yesterday. Did you find enemies?"

"Hey! Yume! Cut that out! There's no need to be nice to the guy!" Ranta yelled.

"It's fine! Don't you feel sorry for him?!" Yume shot back.

"No, Yume. Ranta's right." Kikkawa looked away, brushing Yume's hand aside. "I don't have any right to have you treat me like that. Enemies, huh. Yeah. There were. Enemies. They didn't even try to communicate. Just attacked us out of nowhere, man..."

As Kikkawa told the story, when the Tokkis had moved away from the hill with white boulders scattered around on it and arrived in the valley where the white pillar-like boulders were the thickest, the enemy had ambushed them.

They had been humanoid; they'd worn white cloths over their heads with holes cut out where their single eyes were, and they'd carried extremely sharp spear-like weapons. They'd also been about the same height as humans.

When they'd seen them, Tada had muttered, "They look like a cult." And so, the Tokkis had taken to calling them cultists.

The cultists had hidden in between the white pillar-like rocks to ambush the Tokkis. Apparently, they had outnumbered them. What was more, because the enemy had the element of surprise, the Tokkis had started out at a disadvantage. Even so, the Tokkis had put up a good fight and killed seven of the cultists. The rest had fled.

On the Tokkis' side, Kikkawa, Inui, and Mimorin had been lightly injured. The Tokkis had two priests, Tada and Anna-san. Tokimune himself was also a paladin, so while he couldn't heal himself, he could heal his comrades' wounds. When they had gone to heal themselves, though... that was when they'd realized it.

"No light magic?" Merry brought a hand to her mouth.

"Yeah, that's right." Kikkawa hung his head. "It didn't work, or it didn't activate? Something like that. Our Protection had worn off at some point, too."

"Now that you mention it...it happened yesterday, too," said Merry slowly. "I noticed it when we went out there. I just thought the duration on it had run out, though."

"Oh..." Ranta's eyes went wide. "Zodiac-kun vanished, too, huh?"

"The gods," Shihoru said in a whisper. "Light magic borrows power from Lumiaris...and dark magic borrows power from Skullhell to produce their effects. That's why."

"It's another world." Merry bit her lip. "The blessings of Lumiaris and the malice of Skullhell don't reach the Dusk Realm."

"Meow..." Yume put her hands on her cheeks. "If that's true, then if anyone gets hurt, Merry-chan won't be healin' them, y'know. That's gonna make it real tough."

"That's terrifying," Kuzaku said simply. As the one who stood on the front line as the party tank, it wasn't just a problem; it was a matter of life and death.

"So, like..." Kikkawa lifted his right hand weakly, then lowered it. "Of course, we panicked. Even though you wouldn't expect it from us. That's when enemy reinforcements...or something like that...showed up."

"Cultists?" Haruhiro asked.

"No, not them," said Kikkawa. "Well, they were there, too. These guys were huge... I dunno how to describe them. Big, white, like statues. They had human bodies, but their heads were like lions'. As for their size... How big were they again? I'd say four meters tall, maybe. Maybe not that much? Could have been three meters."

"White giants..." Haruhiro said slowly.

"That's right," said Kikkawa. "There were three of those...guys? Or things? Whichever. Along with a whole pile of cultists. Well, we ran, of course. Not like there was much choice. So, like, there was the rubble of some kinda building? A ruin? Something like that. It was, like, crazy big. We fled into there, but they just wouldn't give up. They chased after us forever. They searched for us, we ran and hid. A number of times, we had to fight them, and so Tokimune-san and Tadacchi got hurt, too. Well, basically everyone but Anna-san was battered and bruised all over."

"You guys really do protect Anna-san," Haruhiro said.

"It's a part of our identity. It's a thing we do." Kikkawa gave a weak laugh. "So, Tokimune-san, he told me to run for it. To go and call for help."

"Now listen..." Ranta said, rubbing his face. "If you tell us all that dangerous stuff, do you think we're really going to go? I mean, even if we wanted to, we couldn't. Everyone has to look out for their own hide, man. Even if, deep down, they want to help..."

"Well, yeah," Kikkawa said to Ranta with upturned eyes. "Listen, Ranta. I know that much. Tokimune-san knows it, too. But, still. It was a question of losing everyone or having just one of us get away, that's what I think. If we'd had to choose just one of us to get out of there, obviously, it would be Anna-san. But Anna-san can't do anything on her own. Still, protecting Anna-san while all of us ran felt like it'd be a bit too much for us. If we did that, in the end, it'd get us all killed. So, with Tokimune-san and Anna-san not being options, as the one who was only lightly injured, and who had the shortest career as a volunteer soldier, I was the one they chose. We were going to risk everything to get one of us out. I just happened to be that one. So, like, with me being the seriously lucky man that I am, I was able to run all this way. But, you know, really...I want to do something to save Tokimune-san and the others. Those guys took me in, man. When I'm with them, I have a crazy amount of fun. I mean, we get along great. Man, I love those guys. That's why—thanks, Haruhiro. And Merry-chan. For healing me. Me, I'm going back."

When Kikkawa tried to stand, Haruhiro blocked his way. He couldn't say, *Hold on.* Haruhiro hadn't decided anything yet.

Options. How many were there?

They could choose to let Kikkawa go alone. In other words, abandon him.

They could choose not to abandon him, and instead go with him.

They could choose to go back to the Lonesome Field Outpost to gather people, then go to help.

Haruhiro thought the third seemed like the best option. Now that it had come to this, it was no time to worry about the knowledge of their discovery, the Dusk Realm, spreading. They needed to give up, accept that, and focus on rescuing the Tokkis. And, well, Haruhiro personally had no issue with that. If it was the sort of place that could easily put the Tokkis in a crisis, it was too much for Haruhiro and his group to handle. But, time.

It would take time.

If they left for the Lonesome Field Outpost now, it would take more than four hours to get there and back. That wasn't counting the time it'd take to get a group of people together. This was the time of day when all of the volunteer soldiers would be out, so it would probably take some work.

The Tokkis had been so pressed that they'd been forced to send Kikkawa off on his own. The sooner help reached them, the better. Or rather, they had no choice but to hurry.

Basically, choosing the third option would be little different from choosing the first. It meant those two were the same option. The question was: Would they abandon Tokimune, Anna-san, Tada, Inui, and Mimorin, or would they go save them right now?

Grimgar of Fantasy and Ash

8. Let's Go Down the Hill

I'm fine with being mediocre. Just let me be more decisive, Haruhiro thought. *I want to become a leader who can make split-second decisions and not leave his comrades feeling uncertain. I probably can't be the sort that makes them think, "I want to follow him," but I want to at least be the kind of leader that makes them think, "Well, I guess I'll follow him."*

That seems pretty hard, though.

One more step, and they would be in the Dusk Realm, and yet Haruhiro's eyes were still looking sleepy. No... He couldn't see them himself, but he knew they probably were. They had to be.

The feeling of tension, the indecision, the regret, the feeling of, *Yeah, let's not do this after all,* and the thought that, *No, we have to do it,* were all getting mixed together. At times like this, Haruhiro's eyes looked even sleepier than usual. He was aware of that himself.

Of course, it wasn't that he was sleepy. He was confident that, right now, even if Shihoru hit him with her Sleepy Shadow spell, he wouldn't feel even the least bit drowsy.

Despite that, his eyes looked sleepy.

He couldn't have looked less prepared.

"My bad, Haruhiro," Kikkawa said, sounding sincerely contrite.

"Well, yeah. This *is* your bad." Ranta gave a nasal laugh. "Let me say, Kikkawa. This favor is gonna cost you big, man. You'd better understand that."

"Oh, stop!" Yume jabbed Ranta in the shoulder. "You shouldn't be sayin' stuff like that. Kikkawa's havin' a really bad time right now."

"Yumecchi..." Kikkawa teared up. It seemed he really was feeling weak right now.

"Magic...is usable," Shihoru said, nodding to Haruhiro. "I can feel the elementals. It's fine."

"I'll defend Shihoru with everything I have." Merry hit the ground with her short staff.

"As for me..." Kuzaku lowered the visor on his close helm. "...I'll protect everyone."

"Let's take it easy." Haruhiro scratched the back of his head. "... Hmm. No, that's not quite right. I'm trying to say don't be so on edge, maybe. I guess that's the same thing. Well, just to make sure I get the point across, don't be reckless. Sorry, Kikkawa, but if things go bad, I plan to pull out. Also, there are a number of points where we have an advantage over the Tokkis."

"We have me! The great Ranta-sama!" Ranta puffed up his chest proudly.

"First, we have information." Haruhiro, naturally, ignored him. "The cultists. The white giants. We know that there are enemies here. We can stay on guard. Kikkawa also remembers the way to the ruins. We're also aware that light magic and, though this one is just an extra, dark magic don't work."

"And we have me!" Ranta spun around and struck a weird pose.

"Also, there are our numbers." Haruhiro, it went without saying, ignored him. "We don't have anyone like Anna-san who needs protecting—okay, that was just a joke, but we do have Kikkawa, so we have one more. Kikkawa, you're a tank, right?"

"Yeah," Kikkawa nodded. "Tokimune-san's a paladin with a shield and everything, but he doesn't feel very tanky, does he? That's why I'm our main tank."

"Well, together with Kuzaku, we'll have two tanks," Haruhiro said. "For now, Kuzaku will be the main, and we'll have Kikkawa be a sub tank."

"Righto," said Kuzaku.

"Okay," said Kikkawa.

"Now, as for the third advantage—"

"It's me, right?!" Ranta burst in.

"Yeah, that's right, it's you, Ranta," said Haruhiro. "We can sacrifice you any time we need to. That's a huge advantage."

"Heh heh heh... Isn't it, though? I mean, I'm—" Ranta stopped. "Wait, sacrifice me?! I oughta sacrifice you! Go die!"

"Also, there's one more advantage," Shihoru said, pointing to Haruhiro. "A cautious leader."

"Huh?" Haruhiro blinked. *Right now, I don't think I have sleepy eyes.*

"Ha ha! Aha ha ha!" Kikkawa, who had been looking depressed all this time, sounded just a little cheerful when he burst into that short laugh. "You can say that again. When we get in our groove and just go boom, boom, boom, we're invincible, but once we get tripped up, well...we can be pretty weak, you know. Harucchi, your party seems pretty stable. Maybe your lack of enthusiasm is a positive there?"

"What's positive about it?!" Ranta hollered, looking ready to puke in distaste. "It's clearly a negative! He's a drag! It's like being at a funeral every day! Try to put yourself in my shoes!"

"It makes it easy on me." Kuzaku slowly turned his head.

"For me, too." Merry raised one hand.

"And me." Shihoru smiled.

"Yume, too. It's easy and breezy, and that's real great, isn't it?"

"The only thing breezy is the inside of your head, Yumeeee!" Ranta yelled. "Only you, with your tiny tits, feel that way!"

"Don't call them tiny!"

"If you don't like it, try rubbing them until they get big!" Ranta hollered.

"When Yume rubs her boobs, she starts feelin' all funny, so no!" she shot back.

"...What, you've actually tried rubbing them?" Ranta asked, startled.

"They're Yume's boobs, if Yume wants to rub them, or do anythin' else to them, that's Yume's business," she snapped back.

"W-well, yeah, but that's not what I meant..."

"Pervert." Merry focused an icy glare on Ranta.

"Deviant." Shihoru looked at Ranta with blatant contempt.

It looks like everyone's starting to get into it.

Though, in truth, Haruhiro had already thought his presence was one advantage they had.

Not as a leader, but as an active thief, and as a scout. Haruhiro himself thought that his personality was a good fit for being a thief. He might not be so great in combat, but in exploration or spying, he figured he might be pretty useful.

Haruhiro's self-appraisal aside, he was happy to receive praise from his comrades. It helped motivate him.

"Harucchi." Kikkawa tapped the back of his gauntleted hand on Haruhiro's shoulder. "I'll leave the call on when to retreat to you, and I'll obey it. For now, you can think of me as one of yours. I may not look it, but I'm pretty useful, you know?"

"I'll be counting on you." Haruhiro punched Kikkawa in the arm. "Okay. I'll take the lead. Everyone, follow behind me at a distance of around ten meters. The marching order will be Kikkawa, Kuzaku, Ranta, Shihoru, Merry, Yume. Yume, watch the rear for me."

"Righty-meow!" she cried.

Once he'd heard Yume's odd reply, Haruhiro started to walk.

He set foot in the Dusk Realm.

The sky that, at first glance, looked like the evening sky, but was actually random colors, hung high above them, and the wind was fairly strong.

This wind is a bit of a problem, he thought. *According to Kikkawa, there weren't enemies around this first hill today, either. Still, a lack of caution could be the death of us. Those pillar-like white rocks scattered around the grass-covered slope are large enough that a person could easily hide behind them. For those pillar rocks, rather than approach them going straight in one direction, it would probably be better to move left and right to eliminate any blind spots. It's not easy, but thinking about what I need to do and how to do it as I walk is pretty fun.*

Haruhiro went down the hill at his normal walking speed. When he turned back, Kikkawa nodded and pointed ahead of him.

Looks like I have the direction right, Haruhiro noted.

They had left their tents, provisions, and heavy equipment just in front of the entrance to the Dusk Realm. Haruhiro and the others were traveling light.

Eventually, when the ground leveled out, Haruhiro felt a certain sense of foreboding. He turned back, looking to the top of the hill he had come down.

Was it needless anxiety?

There are enemies up the hill. That idea had flashed through his mind, but there were none there. *This time, it was my imagination, but it's far better to wear myself out with unwarranted anxiety than to be careless and let the enemy catch us unaware. I'm gonna take every caution and be overanxious like crazy.*

Eventually, they reached a point where there were hardly any of the pillar rocks.

However, he still hadn't spotted anything resembling a tree. Were there no trees in this world?

Haruhiro would occasionally turn back, checking with Kikkawa that he was heading in the right direction.

"That's bizarre..." he muttered, then exhaled.

It was as bright as evening, but there was nothing like a sun.

There were no birds or bugs flying around. There was no sound of wind. When he turned around for somewhere between the tenth and twentieth time, Haruhiro noticed something was off. But, as for what that was, he wasn't sure.

Still, it bothered him. He signaled with his hands for everyone to come to a stop.

He looked around.

Where is it? What...?

Haruhiro gulped. *Is that it?*

The pillars on that initial hill, he thought. *Not all of them. Only a few.*

Haruhiro squinted his eyes. There was no doubt about it.

They're moving.

The rock pillars, maybe one in ten of them, they're slowly—honestly, it's just a little bit at a time—moving around.

Now, if someone had asked him, *So what?*, he wouldn't have known what to say. If he were asked what they were, and what it meant, Haruhiro would have no answer. However, the fact of the matter was, for at least some subset of them, while he couldn't be sure they were alive, he could be sure they were moving. They were able to move.

"That's really bizarre," Haruhiro muttered.

Should I explain to my comrades? he wondered. *Maybe not yet. If the pillar rocks all moved, that would mean we couldn't navigate by them, which would be a problem. That doesn't seem to be the case, so it isn't an issue—I think.*

Ranta raised both his hands to the side, shrugging his shoulders as if to say, *What's up?*

Nothing. Haruhiro shook his head in response. *The first thing, or rather, the only thing, we need to focus on is heading for the ruins. We shouldn't think about anything but rescuing the Tokkis while avoiding danger as much as possible.*

Haruhiro advanced forward. It was smooth, but there were a lot of ups and downs. In the places where it was higher or lower, he often saw the pillar rocks.

It seems the pillar rocks don't like level ground, Haruhiro thought. Then he realized he was viewing the pillar rocks as something close to living creatures. *Whatever the case, it's probably best not to get too close to the pillar rocks.*

But, as soon as he made that decision, there was a dog.

It was sudden, but it seemed so natural. It was lying low in the grass, wagging its tail, and it wasn't that close, so, *Huh...* was all he thought. He wasn't particularly shocked. At first, that was.

Hey, wait, he quickly reconsidered. *This is the Dusk Realm. Another world. It's weird that there's a dog—or at least, I can't say that for sure, but I should be suspicious of it.*

Well, on closer inspection, it wasn't a normal dog at all. It was somewhere between a large and medium sized dog. It looked like a dog with long, white fur, but it wasn't clear whether it was really a dog. Actually, it probably wasn't what you'd usually call a dog.

This pseudo-dog—it only had one eye. If Haruhiro were to give it a name, he'd call it a one-eyed dog.

This was something he had no choice but to stop for. The others had stopped walking, too. Well, now what?

The one-eyed dog looked in their direction, its posture low and its tail wagging, like a friendly dog that had found people in an uninhabited field and wanted to play. That was what it acted like. But it had only one eye.

If it wasn't going to attack, could they leave it be? But that friendliness made Haruhiro think something was up. Could it be the cultists' dog? Might it let the cultists know about Haruhiro and the others? Or was he overthinking things? Was he being needlessly anxious?

He decided to wait and see what it did. While motioning for his comrades to come in closer, Haruhiro watched the one-eyed dog. The one-eyed dog didn't move.

"Never seen one of those before," Kikkawa whispered. "Oh, but, now that I think about it, if I recall, the cultists only had one eye hole, and the lion-headed white giants—they only had one eye, too."

"Then this guy's with them?" Ranta went to draw Betrayer.

"Either that," Shihoru began hesitantly, "or it's possible all the creatures in this world...have just one eye..."

"It's kind of creepy." Merry sounded dubious. "The way it's wagging its tail."

"It's like a pet dog, isn't it?" Kuzaku was apparently thinking along the same lines as Haruhiro.

"This's a job for Yume," Yume declared, proudly thumping her chest. "Yume's a hunter, after all. Yume's gonna try and get up close, so everyone keep an eye on it."

Haruhiro decided to let Yume handle it. Of course, he got ready to jump in and help at any moment.

"Ahem." Yume cleared her throat loudly, then slowly approached the one-eyed dog. It was a slow, easy pace, but it was kind of...normal. Yume didn't particularly try to make eye contact with the one-eyed dog, or stick out her hand and try to present a friendly attitude. It was so normal, Haruhiro had to wonder, *Is this going to be okay?*

The one-eyed dog was staring at Yume with its single, but large eye.

What was the one-eyed dog thinking as it stuck out its tongue, panting?

There were about four meters between them.

"Easy, easy," Yume said, talking to the one-eyed dog for the first time. "It's okay. Yume's not gonna do anythin' bad to you."

The one-eyed dog didn't respond. It just kept staring at Yume.

Three more meters. Two meters.

That was when the one-eyed dog got up from the down position and sat.

Yume started to stop, but then kept moving forward. Lowering her hips, she slowly approached the one-eyed dog and stuck out her hand.

"Paw."

"O, o, o, o, o!"

That voice. Based on the fact that it had opened its mouth, it had probably been the one-eyed dog that made the noise. It was rather low in tone, an eerie voice.

Yume let out an "Eek...!" and stopped walking.

"O, o, o, o, o!"

"That's scary!" Ranta half drew Betrayer.

In that instant, the one-eyed dog turned and started to race off.

"Ah!" Haruhiro gave chase. "No, we can't let it get away!"

"Ohm, rel, ect, nemun, darsh!"

At the same time as Haruhiro went to chase the one-eyed dog—perhaps sooner—Shihoru began chanting a spell. The shadow elemental flew forth, fixing itself to the ground right in the path of the fleeing one-eyed dog. The one-eyed dog stepped on the shadow elemental with its right front paw.

"O, o, o, o...!"

Struggle as it might, the one-eyed dog couldn't free its paw from the shadow elemental.

"W-wait!" Yume tried to stand in Haruhiro's way. "Not yet! It's just runnin'. That doesn't make it an enemy!"

"Sorry, Yume!" Haruhiro walked past her. "We can't take risks here! No, actually…"

"O, o, o, o, o, ooooooooooo!"

The one-eyed dog was struggling violently.

But that's not all, Haruhiro thought. *There's something…coming out of it, I think?*

They were growing out of its body here and there. White, bone-like protrusions with sharp tips.

"Eeeek!" When Yume turned and saw them, she let out a shriek. "Scary, scary, scary! That's no doggie!"

"Damn straight." Ranta lowered the visor on his skull helm. Using Leap Out, he sprung towards the one-eyed dog. "Take this! Hatred!"

"O, o, o, ooooo!"

The one-eyed dog couldn't run away thanks to Shihoru's Shadow Bond. Still, it contorted its body. Ranta had probably meant to split the one-eyed dog's head open with Betrayer, but he missed his mark. The sword struck one of the bone-like growths coming out of the one-eyed dog's shoulder, and was deflected.

"Whoa?! That's hard!" Ranta leapt back.

"I'll do it!" Kuzaku charged forward with his shield in front of him.

Kuzaku's shield and the one-eyed dog's bone-like growths collided. The one-eyed dog lost the pushing contest, but there was an intense screeching. Kuzaku's kite-shaped heater shield was made of wood and reinforced with leather and metal. It was a sturdy piece of equipment. It didn't break, but the surface was scraped off.

"Hah!" Kuzaku didn't care. He just continued to push in and thrust his longsword out from beside his shield. While protecting himself with the shield, he used Thrust. It was a basic tactic for paladins.

The one-eyed dog cried "O, o, o!" and tried to avoid the longsword. Those bone-like things were in the way, but the longsword weaved between them to strike at the one-eyed dog's body. Its blood was red.

Haruhiro decided not to charge in, instead keeping an eye on the situation. A straight-up melee wasn't a thief's place anyway.

"Aw, yeah!" Kikkawa slammed his bastard sword into the one-eyed dog. The one-eyed dog had been preoccupied with Kuzaku, so it took the full force of this blow.

"Heh heh heh!" Ranta bounced around using Leap Out to get around to the side of the one-eyed dog, then swung Betrayer in a figure-eight pattern. "My super deadly attack! Slice!"

"Oooo, oo, oooooo, oooooo...!"

The one-eyed dog was bloodied in an instant. No matter how fierce it was, if its movements were sealed with magic and it was surrounded by a paladin, a warrior, and a dread knight, it was going to have a hard time.

The one-eyed dog collapsed in short order, but until it stopped twitching, Ranta stubbornly continued to stab it. It was cruel, but they couldn't afford to take half measures.

"A perfect victory! Am I right?!" Ranta raised his visor, flashing a sinister smile in Yume's direction. "That was one hell of a pup! Ga ha ha ha!"

"That thing wasn't a doggie!" Yume's cheeks were puffed up in anger.

"...Still." Shihoru glanced to Haruhiro. "What if...there were a whole bunch of these things..."

"No question, we'd be in trouble," Haruhiro said with a glance at the one-eyed dog's remains. "It looked fast. If a big pack of these one-eyed dogs were chasing us, it'd be pretty rough."

Oh, not good, he realized. *Everyone's gone quiet.*

"W-well." Haruhiro forced a smile. "It's a good thing. We've found out there're creatures like this one here. I mean, now that we know, there're countermeasures we can take."

Were there really, though? He couldn't think of any at the moment.

Damn it, he thought. *This is scary. The Dusk Realm is beyond crazy.*

Haruhiro pulled out a canteen and took a drink of water, and each of his comrades rehydrated themselves, too, as if following his example.

Calm down. No, I am calm. I'm not panicking.

When he looked over to Kikkawa, the man was hanging his head. He probably felt bad for getting them involved in this.

That's true, yeah? Haruhiro thought. *If someone said he got us wrapped up in this, that much might be true. But we had the option of not getting involved. We just didn't choose to take it. That's not Kikkawa's fault.*

Did I make the wrong decision?

There's scarcely a day when I don't ask myself that question. In fact, I've made the wrong decisions more than a few times. I'm always making mistakes.

I go on making mistakes, never learning, but still, somehow, we're here today, and I know I have no choice but to move forward. Even if the choices I make are wrong, I have to move forward without a word about it. If I don't, then everyone will be at a loss for what to do.

"Okay," Haruhiro said. "Let's go."

Haruhiro started to walk, then quickly looked around the area. *This is bad. Like, seriously.*

This is crazy.

"O, o, o, o..."

"O, o, o, o, o, o..."

"O, o, o..."

"O, o, o, o, o, o, o, o..."

With that creepy growl, one-eyed dogs with those bone-like protrusions were closing in on them.

From there, and over there, too, he thought, alarmed. *At a quick count, there are four of them. No...*

"O, o..."

"O, o, o..."

"O, o, o, o..."

"O, o, o, o, o..."

"O, o, o, o, o, o..."

From behind, another five. That makes nine, total... For now.

Haruhiro couldn't be sure there weren't more coming.

"Hey, Paropiruro..." Ranta was sounding uncharacteristically unenthusiastic.

"What is it, Rantanius?" That lame comeback was a clear indication that Haruhiro was far from calm.

"So, how about those countermeasures?" Ranta asked. "You've got some, right...?"

"Y-yeah..." If Haruhiro just confessed *I've got nothing,* it felt like that would be easier. But it'd only be easier on Haruhiro; the rest of them would suffer. That was no good. He was the leader, after all.

"F-fall back," he said. He immediately questioned, *Is that going to be okay?* but Haruhiro shook off his hesitance. "Form a circle. Fall back. Oh, I guess in a circle, there is no back, huh? Erm, I'll give orders for the direction, so go where I say. Quickly. Get into a circle. Hurry, Ranta, Kuzaku, Kikkawa! Yume, don't you dawdle, either! Shihoru and Merry, get in the center!"

Haruhiro, Ranta, Kuzaku, Kikkawa, and Yume got in a formation around Shihoru and Merry.

There were now nine one-eyed dogs surrounding Haruhiro and the others. Though, that said, it wasn't as if the one-eyed dogs had formed a ring around them with equal distance between each of them.

Haruhiro chose to break out through one of the openings. Haruhiro and the others advanced in that direction. They didn't run. With weapons out, shields at the ready, they advanced at slower than a walking pace while intimidating the one-eyed dogs.

"Hey! Heyyy!" Ranta kept shouting and swinging Betrayer. "D-don't you come any closer, you mutts! I'll kill you, dammit!"

"Ha ha ha. Man..." Kikkawa looked dispirited. "I dunno what to make of this. I'm beat."

"We'll get through somehow." It was hard to tell if Kuzaku was feeling confident or not. "...Probably."

"Nnyoahhhhhhhh." Yume had nocked an arrow to her composite bow, and seemed to be struggling to decide whether to let it loose or not. "Yume's gonna end up hatin' doggies. Even though these aren't doggies..."

"H-how far will we go like this...?" Shihoru asked.

Was she asking Haruhiro that, maybe? There was no way he could answer.

"If we have to fight, we fight," Merry said.

That's right, Haruhiro thought. *Do we fight? Do we just fight? Are we gonna fight? It's fine, right? We might be able to manage it. If we go at it with everything we have, try our hardest, we may win.*

"May, *huh?*" Haruhiro ground his back teeth. *It's no good.* "May" *isn't good enough. Even if we win, what if one of us gets seriously wounded? We can't heal. In fact, even if we keep moving like this, is there any hope that the situation will get better? What will the one-eyed dogs do? When will they strike? Or will they give up?*

What should we do?

Haruhiro was always making mistakes, but this time, he couldn't afford to get it wrong.

What will we do?

9. Unwanted Help

This way. It's this way. This way. Over here. This way...

Haruhiro just kept giving directions. No one else was saying anything anymore.

"O, o, o, o, o, o..."

"O, o, o, o, o, o, o, o, o, o..."

"O, o, o, o..."

"O, o, o, o, o, o, o..."

The one-eyed dogs growled. Sometimes, they'd howl loudly, too.

How far have we come from that initial hill? How many minutes have passed since we were surrounded by dogs? Is it a time that can be counted in minutes? Ten minutes? Fifteen minutes? Twenty minutes? I don't know.

Did Haruhiro's eyes look sleepy now? Almost certainly. His eyes must have looked pretty sleepy.

Thi-this is tough, he thought. *My heart feels ready to give out. I can't breathe well. I'm sweating like crazy. It feels gross. My legs are ready to give out, too. I'm amazed that I can still walk at all. It's a wonder to me how I'm managing to.*

However, the one-eyed dogs would leap at Haruhiro and the others, and then back away, as if keeping a fixed distance—that was what Haruhiro was thinking. It was about two meters. Out of range of the party's weapons.

It was questionable if Haruhiro and the party could keep moving. True, the one-eyed dogs' encirclement of them was loose, but it also felt like they were breaking the circle in response to Haruhiro and the others' moving.

These things are cautious. To an almost cowardly degree. They won't attack easily, he thought. *There's a depression up ahead. A valley. With lots of pillar rocks. The Tokkis were ambushed by cultists in a valley that was dense with pillar rocks. I don't want to go into the valley.*

Haruhiro took a deep breath. "Ranta, Kuzaku, Kikkawa. You three, work together to kill one of them quickly. Shihoru, use magic. Thunderstorm. Yume, use arrows. Make sure you hit. If we can take out several of them in an instant, the rest will turn tail and run. We're gonna do it. Got it? Shihoru's magic will be the signal to go."

Will these things turn tail? Do I have any guarantee? No. Am I confident? No. But I have no choice but to state it like a fact here. No, it's what I should do. That's why I did it. This is good.

Ranta pointed at the one-eyed dog in front of him with Betrayer.

Yume drew back on her bowstring.

"Jess, yeen, sark..." Shihoru began to chant.

It's looking good. This is a good flow. We didn't work out the fine details, but we're acting in sync. Things work out when we're like this.

"Kart, fram, dart...!"

There was a flash of light. Then a roaring sound. A bundle

of lightning fell. Shihoru caught three of the one-eyed dogs in Thunderstorm's effective range. The one-eyed dogs were blasted away without so much as a cry.

Yume released her bowstring. Haruhiro leapt forward.

"Okay!" Kuzaku went, too.

He charged in with his shield, knocking over the one-eyed dog Ranta had pointed at. That one-eyed dog immediately tried to get back up, but Ranta and Kikkawa were having none of that.

Ranta bellowed and Kikkawa shouted, "Here goes...!"

Yume's arrow stabbed into one of the one-eyed dogs' flanks, but that wasn't going to be enough to kill it.

That's fine. It's not a problem. It's already accounted for. Haruhiro closed in on the one-eyed dog. This wasn't a skill he used often, and it had been a while, but he committed to it here.

"Assault!"

He released his internal limiter. That was the image. He stabbed and slashed like crazy with the dagger in his right hand, and bludgeoned it like a madman with the sap in his left. He didn't breathe. He had stopped.

Do it. Do it. Do it. Do it. Do it. Just do it!

Haruhiro wasn't even viewing the one-eyed dog as a living creature. It was a thing. He wasn't so much killing it as smashing it apart. He'd crush it to a fine pulp.

Even when the one-eyed dog went down, Haruhiro didn't let up. Yume put an arrow in another one-eyed dog that tried to leap at Haruhiro. The arrow caused that one-eyed dog to back down.

Haruhiro remained focused on the task of destroying the one-eyed dog in front of him. Kuzaku and Ranta were getting started on their second dog. Kikkawa took a swing at the one that tried to attack Haruhiro—the one Yume had hit with an arrow. Haruhiro was keeping track of the situation out of the corner of his eye and in one corner of his mind, but he had no intention of stopping until his target was completely destroyed.

That target soon fell silent.

"O, o, o, o, o...!"

The remaining one-eyed dogs ran away. Of the three dogs that had been struck by Shihoru's Thunderstorm, one of them got up and chased after its pack.

Haruhiro was winded. He had no strength left. He felt incredibly exhausted. He wanted to sit down and rest. Or rather, to sleep. He wanted to take a nap, maybe two naps. Of course, that wasn't going to be an option.

"We're getting out of here!" he shouted.

They'd managed to drive off the one-eyed dogs. From the looks of things, no one had been injured. Even Haruhiro, tired as he was, was unharmed.

They had accomplished their goal. Though it had only been a minor goal. The major goal was rescuing the Tokkis. They had to go. Now was the time to move forward.

"Uh, let's see..." Kikkawa was looking around restlessly.

Damn it, Haruhiro thought. *He must have lost track of where we were while we were moving around surrounded by the one-eyed dogs.*

Haruhiro wiped the sweat from his face with his hand. *Wh-what now?*

We've got to do something. But how?

It doesn't matter. Pick a direction, any direction—no, bad idea, that won't work, but what do we do?

"Ah!" Kikkawa shouted, pointing off in some direction. "There! There it is! The remains of the buildings...that ruin-like place! That's it!"

Haruhiro looked over in that direction. *Yeah. There it is. It's true.*

"L-let's go!" he called.

I stuttered. But what of it? It's no big deal. Don't sweat it.

It was entirely possible that the one-eyed dogs would come back with friends. Just to be safe, Haruhiro kept some of his attention focused on the direction the one-eyed dogs had fled as the party made their way towards the ruins.

Things were a bit of a mess at first, but they were able to recover while walking at a fast pace. Haruhiro wasn't in great condition himself, but he wasn't in bad shape, either. At the very least, he wasn't breathing raggedly anymore.

If he were to describe the ruins with one word, it would be "white." From a distance, they looked like a white hill, but it was bumpy, and from that it was possible to tell there were buildings lined up there.

As Kikkawa had told them, it was a large area. Like a town made up of nothing but white buildings.

A white town.

If the Tokkis are still there, can we find them? Will we be able to meet up? As they drew closer, Haruhiro became more and more uncertain. *I can see why Kikkawa called this white town a ruin. True, that's not a building. Probably, there was an unimaginably large white building here at one point—how long ago is unclear. That building, whether due to the passage of time, or because something happened, collapsed. The roof and walls fell in, were demolished, the pieces scattered, and the support pillars broken. The majority of the furniture has rotted away, leaving some small traces, and there are shards of statues and tableware scattered around. They're all incredibly large.*

This was likely a building for giants to live in.

Because the building materials were pure white, and because of the unique scale of the building, the word "temple" came to mind.

A giants' temple—that was what this place was.

If so, I guess we should call it the Giants' Temple Ruins.

Well, all of that was only Haruhiro's imaginings. He might be completely off base, but that was the impression he had.

Haruhiro and the others looked up to the now-slanted pillars, as well as the ones supporting them, though both types would have more accurately been described as broken pillars. The space between them was something like a gate. It was more than ten meters high, and about as wide.

The scale was impressive. It made him feel incredibly tiny, and Haruhiro stood there for a few seconds staring vacantly at it. He really *was* tiny.

"Do we...go in...?" Shihoru asked timidly.

"W-we came all this way." Ranta, despite being Ranta, was hesitant. "Not going in would be, well, y'know. Right? That sort of you-know-what stuff is you-know-what. You know what I mean. What's the word? 'Awkward,' right? Basically. Don't you think so?"

"All you keep sayin' is you-know-what." Yume seemed relatively fine with the situation. "Still, sure is big, huh? Yume may never've seen anythin' so big before."

"If we were here for sightseeing..." Kuzaku lifted his visor and squinted his eyes, "...it'd be a fun place to check out."

"You might be right." Merry smiled slightly.

"When it comes to the inside, guys," Kikkawa said apologetically, "honestly, I don't remember it so well. Sorry. I had bigger concerns at the time. But I don't think we went in too deep. Like, when I came out of here, it didn't take me that long."

"Cultists and white giants, huh?" Haruhiro took a deep breath. "No, we'd better assume there could be more than that. There were the one-eyed dogs, after all."

"Actually, it looks like there's more than just them." Ranta gestured up and to the left with his chin.

When Haruhiro looked, there was something on top of one of the broken pillars.

White. Of course it's white—an ape? Is that what it is? At a glance, it looks like a little white hairless ape, but with only one eye.

"Meow..." Yume readied her bow. "What do you want to do? At this distance, Yume thinks she can probably hit it."

"No." Haruhiro quickly shook his head. "Don't. Not for now..."

There's more than one of the one-eyed apes, he thought. *There's one on top of that broken pillar, too, and another one on top of that mountain of rubble. If I can spot three this quickly, there must be more around. What's more, they're up high enough only arrows or magic can hit them.*

"Kikkawa, have you seen those apes before?" Haruhiro asked.

"Nope," Kikkawa said. "Oh, but maybe we just didn't notice them. We don't really focus on that stuff much, see. How should I put it? If something's not coming at us, we tend to ignore it."

"These temple ruins—that's what I'll be calling them, by the way— when you fought the cultists and white giants in here, were there any other creatures?"

"All I saw were the cultists and the white giants," said Kikkawa. "I dunno what happened after I broke off from the group, though, so I can't say if it's still that way."

"Got it."

It's one decision after another. I think I'll have to get used to it. Getting used to it can lead to lowering my guard. But if I don't get used to it, I can't keep this up.

"We'll ignore the one-eyed apes," said Haruhiro. "Let's go inside."

We're walking side-by-side with danger here, thought Haruhiro as he moved forward. *It's life or death.*

What Kuzaku had said about this being a fun place to go sightseeing crossed Haruhiro's mind. He totally agreed. He'd never seen anything like this place before. It was beyond anything he had imagined. If he were a tourist, he would be in awe of the sights.

Haruhiro went ahead of the group to confirm it was safe, then the other six followed after him.

To confirm it was safe.

Is that even possible? he wondered.

He was doing the best he could, as far as he was concerned, but he still wasn't confident. The truth was, he wanted to be one hundred percent certain it was safe before leading his comrades in there. However, realistically, that wasn't something he could do. It was impossible.

He stepped on the grass, over the white fragments, between the broken pillars. There wasn't anything hiding in the shadows of the broken pillars.

I don't think there is, he added to himself. *But, deeper in, I can't be so sure.*

He couldn't circle a full three hundred and sixty degrees around every single obstacle. It would take forever.

Is eighty percent good enough? Is seventy percent? Or fifty? he wondered. *It's not something you can represent with a number. But, well, I think it's fine. Even though, with that degree of certainty, that's far from certain.*

He passed through the gate of broken pillars and beyond there, on both sides, there were large fragments piled up into walls. In some ways, it was like they were forming a path. However, while he might have called them walls, they were full of gaps. If something was hiding in them, it would be hard to notice.

It makes me want to cry. But I'm not going to. Haruhiro let out a long breath. *For now, I'll do the best that I can do. I can't do what I can't do, after all. There's no helping that.*

Haruhiro used Sneaking to progress along the right-hand side. Weapons drawn. Checking the gaps as best he could. Carefully. But not too carefully. It was fine to be cautious, but excessive timidity was no good.

Don't stop, he told himself. *Even if it's scary, don't be afraid. The one-eyed apes aren't attacking. There's no sign of them following me, either.*

Any sounds? He felt like he could hear something, but he wasn't sure.

The wall ended—or rather, it opened up, forming something like a four-way junction. He gathered everyone there.

"Haruhiro-kun, are you okay?" Shihoru asked.

"Huh? What? Why?" he stammered.

"Your face's color..."

"It's not looking good?" he asked.

"Ohh!" Ranta looked at Haruhiro's face and sneered. "Man, you're really something. Was your skin always that white? You're looking pale. Eh heh heh heh."

"Haru-kun," Yume said with a serious expression, and suddenly squeezed Haruhiro's hand. "Yume knows it must be hard, but you're doin' your best."

"...S-sure," Haruhiro said.

"Man, I've gotta bow my head to you, seriously..." Kuzaku said, and then did exactly that. "It's scary, man. Going ahead by yourself, in a place like this. I couldn't do it."

"R-really? You think...?" Haruhiro asked.

"Haru. If you get tired, tell me," Merry said, practically glaring at him. "Please."

"...If I get tired, sure."

"Then the great Ranta-sama will take your place!" Ranta announced.

"That, I'm gonna say no to."

"An immediate refusal?! Why?!" Ranta shouted.

"Well..." Kikkawa patted Ranta on the shoulder. "That goes without saying, man. Doesn't it?"

It was only for a little while, but everyone laughed. That was enough to let Haruhiro recover, at least mentally.

I'm so simple, he thought. *Not just simple, but an embarrassing guy who's easily swept along. I'm close to getting giddy just from this. I won't, though. That wouldn't be good. If I get complacent, I feel like I'll fail.*

While at the four-way junction, considering which way to go—

I think I may love them, Haruhiro thought. *I think I may love this party of mine. Not Ranta, though. But, well, he's like a little spice thrown into the mix. Probably. Ranta is Ranta, and in his own way, we'd be in trouble without him.*

Still, thinking about how he liked his comrades... Haruhiro really *was* an embarrassing guy. It wasn't a bad thing, mind you, but it sure was embarrassing. Also, Haruhiro thought it didn't suit him. *Thinking I love my comrades. It's not who I am, you know? I'm more of a, well, noncommittal sort of guy, in all sorts of ways, right...?*

"We'll start by going right," he said.

It wasn't intuition. Haruhiro didn't have a natural intuition, like, say, Tokimune did. Haruhiro and the party had come this far following the right-hand wall. If they turned right at the junction, they could continue following the right-hand wall. That was his only reason. If they found nothing, they could just turn back and take another route.

He wanted to hurry as much as possible, but they had no real leads, so they had to search the slow and steady way. And, while Tokimune may not have been the type to do it that way, Haruhiro was.

They moved forward again with Haruhiro leading the way and the rest of the party following behind him. Up until a few moments ago, honestly, he'd been pretty worn out, but he was fine now.

I'll probably stay fine for a while. I can't get overconfident, though. Haruhiro didn't have the skill necessary to get away with being overconfident.

The gaps in the wall...there were more now than before, and they were bigger. More than just hide—a person could go *inside* them. If the Tokkis were all right, it might be because they had fled through one such gap.

When Haruhiro progressed another two, three meters, the path turned to the left. Past here, there were a lot of broken pillars and other rubble, and while it was possible to keep going, visibility ahead was not good. It was clearly dangerous.

But he heard a sound.

Haruhiro lowered his eyes and listened closely. He heard the sound of his comrades' footsteps. Then, some other sound.

"...A voice," he murmured.

It was a human voice, probably. Haruhiro raised his face. He turned back. His eyes met with his comrades'. It seemed they hadn't noticed yet.

"Someone's here," he said.

"I'll take point!" Kikkawa rushed forward, getting ahead of Haruhiro.

Haruhiro looked into his comrades' eyes. They had come this far. Having gone to all this trouble, he wanted to rescue the Tokkis. Everyone else should have felt the same.

They followed after Kikkawa in the order of Haruhiro, Kuzaku, Ranta, Merry, Shihoru, and Yume. Kikkawa was fast. He was in too much of a rush. But it was hard to blame him. All they could do now was run, weaving between the obstacles that obstructed their line of sight.

There was a muffled shout from Kikkawa, like he'd started to call out, then stopped himself. He must have wanted to call his comrades' names. To tell them he was here, that he'd come to save them. But the situation was still an unknown. It wasn't even certain that the Tokkis were really here. It was too soon to shout.

"We're almost there!" Haruhiro called out.

He didn't know whether Kikkawa could hear him or not. But it was only a little further. He could hear a voice.

"Nghrahhhh...!"

It was a familiar voice.

"Tadacchi!" Kikkawa shouted. "It's me, Tadacchi! It's Kikkawa! Everybody's friend, Kikkawa, is back! And guess what, guess what! Harucchi and his buds are here, too! Tadacchiiiiiiiii!"

"Gwohrahhh! Zwahhhhh! Nuwagrahhhh...!"

Tada's roaring, Haruhiro thought. *He's probably not in a position to respond. He's in battle, huh. Fighting enemies. That was what it sounds like.*

Kikkawa raced through the rubble and between the broken pillars. Haruhiro raised his speed and caught up to right behind Kikkawa.

Haruhiro saw him.

Tada.

"Wahhrahhh! Fwahhhhhgrah! Zwahhhhhh...!"

Tada was swinging his warhammer around wildly, against humanoids wearing big white sheet-like things over their heads and using spear-like weapons.

Those are the cultists, huh, Haruhiro thought. *There are four of them. Four against one.*

However, it looked like it hadn't always been four against one. There were two downed cultists.

Then, there was that ponytail. That leather, jumpsuit-like outfit. Over by the two fallen cultists, that was...

"Inui-san!" Kikkawa cried, taking a swing at one of the cultists. "You're not getting away with this! Wahhhhhhhhhh!"

Now it was four against two. Tada was still surrounded by three cultists. Tada's priest outfit, his face, and even his glasses were covered in blood.

Haruhiro took up position behind one of the cultists. A thief's job was to stay quiet and use Backstab. He closed in, and his dagger—did not stab into the cultist's back.

"Huh?!" Haruhiro leapt back.

The cultist turned to face in his direction. What was that white cloth-like stuff the cultists were wearing? What was with the way it had felt?

The cultist thrust a spear at him.

Swat. Would he use his dagger or sap to hit it? No—Haruhiro chose to dodge instead.

That white cloth. It was no simple cloth. That being the case, their spears might not be ordinary, either. He needed to be careful.

"Blades!" Tada roared as he swung his warhammer around wildly, "They don't go through it well! Mwahhhh! Fugahhhhhhhhh...!"

"Seriously?!" Kuzaku shouted as he slammed into a cultist with his shield.

"Hmm." Ranta came to a sudden stop. "Guess swords aren't gonna work against them, huh?"

"You dummy!" Yume planted a spinning kick on Ranta's back.

"Urgh!" Ranta closed in on Yume threateningly. "What're you doing?!"

"What's a Wyoming?!" she shouted. "Stop talkin' nonsense!"

"You're the one who never makes sense!"

The idiot was doing as idiots do, but for now, Tada, Kikkawa, Kuzaku, and Haruhiro each took a cultist, turning it into four one-on-one battles.

No, Tada must be just barely holding out, Haruhiro thought. *We need to let him rest.*

"Ranta!" Haruhiro narrowly avoided a sharp thrust from his cultist. "That's enough! Switch with Tada! Hurry!"

"Oh, fine, if you insist!" Ranta tried to rush over to Tada.

"You're a nuisance! Stay away!" Tada declared as he swatted aside the cultist's spear and went on the attack. He attacked, and attacked, and attacked like crazy.

"You heard the man!" Ranta hollered.

"Fine, then choose Kikkawa, or Kuzaku, or even me, but get in here and help someone!" Haruhiro yelled back. "Can't you think for yourself, you moron?!"

"Who're you calling a moroooooooooon?!" Ranta leapt at the cultist who was trying to attack Haruhiro with his spear. "Call me a genius! A great genius!"

The cultist took a hit to the right shoulder from Ranta's Betrayer, but, as expected, it couldn't cut through. The cultist stumbled for a moment, but that was all. No, the cultist did turn in Ranta's direction after that, so maybe he did accomplish a little more than that.

Haruhiro put some distance between himself and the cultist. *What is that?* he thought. *That white cloth. It's not cloth. It seems thicker. It's not hard. It's soft. It felt squishy. Is it some material that doesn't exist in Grimgar? It just looks like they're wearing white sheets over their heads, but are those actually proper coats? They could be armor; they even have proper sleeves. They're long. They go all the way down to their knees. They're wearing white shoes on their feet, too, of course. Those shoes look like they're the same material.*

There's a hole where their eyes should be. Are the cultists one-eyed? Well, that doesn't really matter. Anyway, that may be their weak point.

Yume was nocking an arrow. She looked to Haruhiro. Should she shoot? Shouldn't she? That was the look on her face. Well... Haruhiro wasn't sure. It seemed like she'd have a hard time hitting those holes on a moving target.

"Haruhiro-kun!" Shiharu held her staff tight in both hands.

Oh, right.

When Haruhiro nodded, Shiharu began to chant while drawing elemental sigils with the tip of her staff. "Ohm, rel, ect, el, vel, darsh!"

It wasn't Shadow Beat. With a *vwong, vwong, vwong,* three shadow elementals that looked like balls of black seaweed appeared instead of just one. It was a higher version of Shadow Beat: Shadow Echo.

The shadow elementals flew forth, coiling around one another as they did. All three slammed into the cultist Kikkawa was fighting. The moment they did, the cultist's entire body began convulsing violently.

It let out a "Guwah..."

"It worked!" Shiharu cried.

With a shout, Kikkawa quickly slammed the bastard sword he held with both hands into the cultist. He couldn't cut him, but he didn't have to. It seemed that coat, or armor, or whatever it was, couldn't completely absorb the blow, so he just had to keep on bludgeoning the cultist over, and over, and over.

"Get him, Kikkawa!" Haruhiro called.

Before Haruhiro had said anything, Kikkawa had already started slamming his bastard sword into the cultist with pure brute force. "Wah, rah, rah, rah, rah, rah, rah, rah, rah, rahhhh!"

Haruhiro lent what little help he could, primarily using the sap in his left hand to slug the cultist.

"Ohm, rel, ect, el, vel, darsh!"

Vwong, vwong, vwong.

Shihoru hit the cultist Tada was facing with Shadow Echo, too.

"I don't...!" Tada swung his warhammer, knocking the cultist's spear from his hands and then kicking him to the ground. Then, he slammed his warhammer down repeatedly. "Want! Your! Help! Dammiiiiiiiiiiiit...!"

As for the remaining two, they just had to gang up on them and beat them senseless.

When there were no cultists left moving, Tada sat down. "Dammit. I'm. Tired. Seriously. Dammit. Idiots. Die. Dammit. What. The. Hell..."

He seemed to be muttering something dangerous in short fragments, but it was a mystery how he still had the strength to speak. His arms and legs didn't seem broken or anything, but Tada was so covered in blood, it was hard to tell where he was injured.

Haruhiro looked down at the cultist corpses and thought, *These guys bleed red, too, huh?* Those coats of theirs weren't torn or cut at all. The coats didn't look damaged at all, but the ground was wet with the red blood that dripped out from underneath them.

Ranta was going around stomping on the heads of the cultists who were presumed dead. He wasn't doing it to desecrate the corpses; he was doing it to confirm they really were dead—or so Haruhiro wanted to believe.

Shihoru, Yume, and Merry exchanged glances. Each wore a slightly different expression, but all of them were disturbed.

Kuzaku lifted the visor of his close helm and sighed deeply.

"Heh..." Kikkawa gave a half-laughing snort, then walked forward unsteadily to that ponytail and leather jumpsuit.

To Inui, who was collapsed, face down, on the ground.

Kikkawa fell to his knees and hung his head.

"...What the hell, man? You can't do this to me. I went and got Haruhiro and the others, just like I was supposed to. After that, this just isn't fair. Inui-san..."

10. Not Special

Haruhiro crouched down next to Kikkawa. He didn't know what to say. He struggled to find the words for a moment, but he knew he wouldn't be able to say the right thing anyway. That was because Haruhiro was mediocre to the core.

Haruhiro reached out, placing a hand on the other man's shoulder gently. "Um..." He shook him. "Inui-san?"

"Wha—" Kikkawa looked at Haruhiro, looked at Inui, back to Haruhiro, back to Inui. "...Huh?"

"Heh." Inui moved his head slightly, looking up at Haruhiro with the eye not covered by an eyepatch. "How did you know...?"

"No, it's not that I knew," said Haruhiro. "You were moving slightly. It made me think, 'Oh, he's alive.'"

"Whaaaaaaaa?!" Kikkawa half jumped to his feet, landing squarely on his backside. "No, no, no waysies?! I was, like, sure you were dead..."

"H-he's alive...?" Kuzaku sounded doubtful.

"The guy's talking, so he's gotta be..." Even Ranta sounded appalled.

"I thought he'd bit the... I mean, passed away, too..." Shihoru muttered bitterly.

"Yeah..." Merry nodded.

"Hey." Yume's eyes were wide. "That's true, but, y'know. Inuin's just real good at it, huh? Playin' dead."

"Huh..." Tada kicked the ground. His shoulders were still heaving with each breath. "You. Think. He'd. Go. Down. So. Easy. Huh?!"

"Heh..." Inui grunted, like usual. "It is the secret ultimate technique of my one-eyed fighting style, Dokuganryu... 'Dying Inui, Making Living Idiots Run.'"

"So, basically, you were just playing dead?!" Ranta flipped him the bird.

"He's. One. Stubborn. Bastard..." Tada's body shook. "Always. Has. Been..."

"Ah..." Haruhiro hurriedly got to his feet. "Ta-Tada-san?!"

Tada fell and turned over.

"Wha, wha, wha, wha, wha?!" Kikkawa wildly gesticulated like a frog as he rushed over to Tada.

Inui tried to rise, but he seemed to be having trouble. "C-can't move... Heh..."

Apparently, Inui wasn't unharmed, and had feigned death only as a last resort.

In the end, until Tada came to (he'd passed out with the whites of his eyes showing), and until Inui was able to get up, the party had no choice but to stay put.

"Me and Inui, we were decoys," Tada told them once he came to, drank some water, and was fully conscious. "It was the only way to protect Anna-san. They got Mimori's leg, so she couldn't run. Me and Inui drew the enemies to us, then Tokimune took Anna-san and Mimori to hide somewhere safe. Well, not that anywhere here can be called safe."

"Then when it comes to where Tokimune went..." Haruhiro held back a sigh, taking a short breath instead. "You don't know, huh?"

"We can go back to where we split up," Tada said.

"Good enough." Haruhiro said that, but he didn't think it would be enough at all. Still, he needed to calm everyone's nerves. Tada and Inui might not have been fatally injured, but they were far from being in top fighting shape.

"Man, you're surprisingly..." Tada began to say, then stopped. "...No. Me and Inui shook off a bunch of enemies. We might run into them on the way there."

"Those white giants, you mean?" Haruhiro asked.

"Yeah. They're sluggish, but big. One hit from them would probably kill you."

"Anything else?" Haruhiro asked.

"After we had Kikkawa run away, a cultist with a sword and shield showed up. You need to watch out for that guy."

"Heh." Inui's lips shook. "One scratch...from his sword...will numb your body. Even if you block, it still...gets you... Heh..."

"Oh?" Ranta suddenly looked serious. "Sounds sweet. That sword. I want it. When we take that guy out, his sword's mine. Got it?"

"You're needlessly resilient, you know that?" Tada said. Even he seemed a little put off by Ranta.

"Well, I don't mind, but..." Haruhiro wasn't able to hold back a sigh this time. "You take him out yourself, man. Do that, and you can have his sword, or anything else of his that you want."

"Nice! That's a promise!" Ranta looked to everyone. "If I kill the guy, I'm taking the sword! Well, even if you guys kill him, I'll still take it, though! Either way, the sword's mine! That's settled!"

Everyone else was in low spirits, but Ranta seemed to have gotten a boost in motivation, so it was probably fine. Or rather, all they could do was leave him to do what he wanted. Though, if Ranta would do them all the favor of dying gloriously as he killed the sword guy, Haruhiro was willing to consider crying for him.

Tada and Inui could walk under their own strength, somehow, but running was out of the question. Merry looked pained by that. It must have been incredibly frustrating for her, as a priest.

The party had to match their speed, which meant they had to go slower. If they had to retreat, it would force a difficult decision upon them. But, if that time came, Haruhiro had made his decision.

He'd be sorry—not that that was going to cut it—but he'd still leave Tada and Inui behind. If Kikkawa said he'd stay behind, he could do as he pleased. While Tada and Inui bought time for them, Haruhiro and the others would get out of there.

Of course, it wasn't something he wanted to do. Haruhiro was praying from the bottom of his heart that they wouldn't find themselves in that situation. Still, he could pray as fervently as he wanted, but if it was going to happen, it would. If it did, it'd be too late to think about it. That was why he'd made the call now, so he'd be ready.

If that time comes, I have to be heartless, Haruhiro told himself. *I can do it. I need to believe that. To make myself believe it, and follow through if necessary.*

Tada and Haruhiro walked side-by-side, with Kuzaku, Kikkawa,

Ranta, Shihoru, Merry, Inui, and Yume following them in that order.

Tada was as bloody as before, but he showed no signs of being in pain or stopping. He was a tenacious guy. It made Haruhiro want to say, *You shouldn't strain yourself,* but the situation was what it was. Not straining himself wasn't going to be an option.

When they proceeded down a path with poor visibility for a while and then turned left, they came to a place where the rubble had formed a sort of roof. Tada went under that roof.

While it might have been called a roof, there was light shining through holes here and there. It wasn't dark, but it still felt oppressive and suffocating. The rubble sometimes blocked their way, or divided the path, making the layout complex. It was like a maze.

"We shook a number of the cultists in here." Tada used his index finger to push up his glasses. "They could still be around. Make sure you're careful."

"Do you know the way?" Haruhiro asked.

"Sort of, yeah."

"...Sort of..." Haruhiro muttered.

"Tadacchi's got a great sense of direction, man," Kikkawa said cheerfully. "It's gonna be kay-o, kay-o! Bably-pro! Huh? Was that one hard to get? Probably!"

Haruhiro couldn't help but think, *Saying "probably" in a silly way isn't going to make anyone feel better,* but it was better than having a dispirited Kikkawa. *Or is it? I'm iffy on that.*

They walked through the maze of rubble, relying on Tada to guide them. They turned left, turned right, and turned around as they walked.

Wait, we turned around?! Haruhiro thought.

"Um, Tada-san," he began.

"What? Make it quick. I'm busy now."

"...Okay, I'll get right to the point then. Are you lost?"

"Me? Get *lost*?" Tada asked, offended.

"Well... If you aren't, then that's fine."

"You're absolutely right," said Tada.

Everyone stopped.

It felt like time itself had stopped. It was so silent that it was almost beautiful.

No, it wasn't beautiful at all.

"I'm lost." Tada shouldered his warhammer, a nasty look on his face. "Is there a problem with me getting lost?"

"He's trying to turn it around on us..." Shihoru muttered in blank amazement.

"That's not it." Tada clicked his tongue. "That's not what I'm doing. I don't need to turn anything around, so it's weird for you to say that, you know?"

"Inui-saaaan," Haruhiro groaned. Arguing with Tada was just going to drive everyone crazy. Haruhiro turned to Inui, who was behind him. "Do you know the way?"

"Heh..." Inui raised two fingers. "There are always two paths..."

"Sure," Merry said, closing her eyes and looking up to the ceiling.

"Meow...?" Yume gulped in anticipation. "What does that mean?"

"One is to confer with your own heart." Inui looked off into the distance. "The other, to confer with the wind. The way is always one of these two paths... Heh..."

"Woo!" Kikkawa excitedly thrust a fist into the air. "So cool! Leave it to Inui-san to say something deep! You're the best! No clue what you mean, though! Aha ha!"

"Our own hearts, huh..." Ranta, being Ranta, seemed to be impressed for some reason. "That's it. Yeah! That's what we've gotta do! Parupiro! Quit wasting time and do that!"

Haruhiro tried listening to the voice in his own heart, but all it said was *I want to punch him,* and that didn't seem like it would help. In other words, this wasn't the time for listening to his heart. He didn't feel much wind in the maze of rubble either, and it wasn't like the wind would actually respond to him anyway. If he started hearing voices on the wind, he'd have to be imagining them.

What he *did* hear wasn't the wind at all, and he wasn't imagining it.

Clack... Clack... Clack...

It was the sound of two hard objects striking one another.

Before Haruhiro could issue a warning, it leapt out from around the corner up ahead.

"Cultist!" Haruhiro shouted.

No, this wasn't just any cultist. Instead of a spear, this one had a mirror-like shield and a sword with a slightly purplish aura around it. That *clack, clack,* sound was apparently coming from the sheath sticking out from under the cultist's coat. That was the sound it made when hitting the rubble.

"It just had to be you, huh?" Tada yelled.

Tada swung down his warhammer, but the sword bearer blocked it with his shield. The sword bearer thrust out his sword. Tada leapt out of the way, of course, but he couldn't brace himself when he landed and lost his balance. Haruhiro wanted to cover him. But the enemy had a shield. He couldn't do it himself.

"I've got this!" Kikkawa literally jumped at the sword bearer. He jumped into the air, then swung down at him from above.

The sword bearer caught Kikkawa's bastard sword with his shield. Without missing a beat, he thrust at him, too. It was the same way he'd attacked Tada. Kikkawa seemed to have anticipated it, because he deftly swept the sword bearer's sword away with the part of the blade closest to the hilt on his bastard sword.

Zong! There was an unpleasant sound.

"The...hell...?!" Kikkawa's whole body trembled, and he almost dropped his bastard sword. Even though he didn't actually drop his weapon, he was still wide open.

The sword bearer thrust at him again. Kikkawa couldn't dodge. He couldn't block with his bastard sword, either. It bit into him. The left side of his chest.

"*Oof!*" Kikkawa trembled again, then was knocked to the ground. As befitted a warrior, Kikkawa was wearing plate armor. The sword didn't manage to run him through, but it left a serious dent.

"Urkh... Kikkawaaaaa!" Tada got back into a fighting stance and swung down his warhammer. He attacked. Attacked unrelentingly.

While the sword bearer was defending himself from Tada's warhammer, the rest of the party got into position to attack.

"I'll go up front!" Kuzaku called. He defended himself with his shield as he took Tada's place.

"The sword! The sword! The sword! The sword!" Ranta hollered. He looked like he planned to position himself to the left side, where the hand the sword bearer held his shield was.

Haruhiro went to take up position behind and to the right—or started to, before he reconsidered.

"Haru!" Merry called.

He turned back.

Behind us, huh? he thought. *There are more coming from behind. Cultists. Those ones are lance bearers, so they look like ordinary cultists. But it isn't just one. There are two—no, three of them.*

This is bad. Beyond bad. We could take four lance bearers, but the sword bearer's here, and he's dangerous. They're trying to catch us in a pincer, so we can't ditch Tada and Inui and run. Huh? Am I out of moves?

Though it was only for a moment, Haruhiro was ashamed to admit his thinking had almost frozen up.

"Ohm, rel, ect, el, krom, darsh!" Shihoru began to chant as she drew elemental sigils with the tip of her staff. A black mist-like shadow elemental erupted from her staff and didn't so much fly as drift towards the new enemies.

It was Sleepy Shadow—only not. This was the upgraded version, Shadow Mist.

The black mist was entering the cultists' garments as if it were being sucked in through their eyeholes, sleeves, and hems.

But, will it work? Haruhiro wondered. *Shadow Mist, like Sleepy Shadow, induces an intense sleepiness in the target. In other words, it's a sleep spell. But, when the enemy knows it's coming, it's not as effective. Unless they don't know we're here, or don't think they'll be hit by magic, it's hard to put them to sleep. That's why its use is limited. Like now, when we're the ones being attacked, it's the sort of spell that's basically useless. Shihoru, of course, probably knows that. Actually, she should know it better than anyone.*

And yet, Shihoru deliberately chose Shadow Mist. *It's not like*

Shihoru, but maybe she's taking a big gamble.

The cultists stumbled, then dropped one after another.

"It's because Shadow Echo was really effective..." Shihoru bowed her head for some reason. "I'm sorry! That's why...I thought they might be weak against Darsh Magic!"

"No?! Y-you don't need to apologize for that, do you?!" Haruhiro's voice cracked a little. "That's amazing, Shihoru! You're a model mage! You really saved us there!"

"S-stop it..." Shihoru shrunk into herself. "It was almost a total coincidence..."

"Heh..." Inui adjusted his eyepatch, without a care in the world. "She's a good woman..."

She is, but, no—seriously, could you not be so random? I want to protest. Haruhiro was feeling peeved.

It was questionable whether Haruhiro had any right to say something like, *Keep your hands off our precious mage. I'd never let a ridiculous guy like you have her. I won't accept it.* He didn't think that he did, but he still felt that way. But, of course, this wasn't the time. He wanted to shut Inui down, but it would have to wait.

"Yume! Inui-san! Finish off the cultists before they can wake up!" Haruhiro called. "Tada-san, Kuzaku, Ranta, keep the sword bearer busy! Kikkawa, you okay?!"

"Y-yeah, somehow!" Kikkawa called. "It hurts, but that's all, I guess?!"

"Okay!" Haruhiro ran forward, attacking one of the cultists that was collapsed in the pile of them.

The minimum, he thought. *I need to take them down in the minimum time possible. This has got to be the spot. It's the only one.*

The hole.

He jammed his dagger as hard as he could into the single eyehole. He twisted and pulled, then stabbed in again.

"Meow-ow!" Yume stabbed her machete into another cultist's eyehole.

"Heh!" Inui did, too.

"Don't—" Haruhiro straddled his cultist and stabbed him again. "—Let your guards down! Until they stop moving—make sure they're good and dead!"

Four times. Five times.

The cultist's limp. Doesn't look like he'll be getting up again. He's dead. I killed him.

"This thing." Yume held up one of the spears the cultists had been holding. "Maybe, do you think it could be useful?"

Haruhiro put his dagger away, nodding, then picked up the spear from the cultist he had killed. Inui smirked, sheathing his sword and picking up a spear.

Kuzaku and the others are struggling even when it's three against one, Haruhiro thought. *Because of the sword bearer's sword. It's a nasty one to deal with. It's hard for Shihoru to use her magic, too, because we'd be in trouble if she hit one of them.*

Well, what about six against one, then?

Haruhiro and Yume, along with Inui, attacked the sword bearer with spears from behind Kuzaku and the others. When the sword bearer blocked the spears with his sword, *zong,* there was an incredible shock that made their brains tremble. But Kuzaku and the others were in front of them, and the spears were long, so there was no real fear of a counterattack.

Even as Haruhiro and the others slowly whittled him down, the sword bearer put up a good fight. It wasn't just that he had a sword and shield in place of a spear. He was probably on a higher level than the ordinary cultists. His easy, fluid movements betrayed no openings, and the way he used his sword and shield was good, too. He was far better at it than Kuzaku, the paladin.

Though, that said, it was six-on-one. The party had a lot of leeway in what they could do, while the sword bearer couldn't drop his guard for a second. Also, Haruhiro, as was his nature as a thief, was watching vigilantly for any opportunity.

That hazy, shining line is something anyone can see, he thought. *To be blunt, it's just a matter of probability. If they do the same thing one hundred, one thousand, ten thousand times, anyone would get better at it. They'd start to see paths that made them say, "If I do this, I'll succeed." In a given situation, with certain conditions, a path that they're confident leads to success will naturally emerge. Could they see that path in a certain form—a line, for instance, once every hundred times, every thousand times, every ten thousand times? Either way, it's a matter of probability.*

The only way to raise the probability is to increase the number of trials. Even if the probability doesn't rise, the more trials there are, the more successes there will be.

Visualize, and continue to take aim. Keep at it, with a sort of indifference, but tenaciously nonetheless.

When I'm taking aim, there's something that looks like a chance every few seconds. I need to accurately judge which of those is a real chance.

Even if it's not a special or unique skill, if I just keep doing this for a while, sometimes I'll see that line.

Look. There it is.

Next time I see it, I can't hesitate. There's no need to think. No need for fear. Just do it. Follow through.

Haruhiro grappled the sword bearer from behind, jabbing the dagger that he was holding with a backhand grip into the eyehole. He pulled it free, then immediately jumped away.

The sword bearer tried to turn around, but Ranta and Kuzaku, along with Tada, all whaled on him and knocked him to the ground.

"Oohohohoo!" Ranta whooped gleefully as he tried to go in for the kill.

"Out of the way, you monkey. Eat—" Tada pushed Ranta aside, winding back with his warhammer before smashing it into the sword bearer's head. "—This!"

He crushed it.

Haruhiro quickly glanced in all directions. They'd taken out all of the cultists. For the moment, it didn't look like any more reinforcements were coming.

Haruhiro must have had sleepy eyes right now. Like always.

That's fine with me, he thought.

"Good work, guys," he said. "Let's move on quickly. Kikkawa, you can move, right?"

"I can...yeah?" Kikkawa was swinging his arm to test that it still worked, and he was on his feet, so, well, he was probably fine. "But can't you be more...I dunno. Nah, that may just be how you are, Harucchi, but when we absolutely nail it like that, doesn't it get you excited? Like, don't you want to shout out 'Hurrah!'?"

"Hurrah."

"Man, that's the most emotionless yippee I've ever heard!" Kikkawa

complained. "It's, like, an ultra-rare hurrah, don't you think?!"

"This is what he's like. Boring! That's what he is!" Ranta snatched that special sword out of the sword bearer's hands. "Hyuk hyuk hyuk! I got me a sword! For the tingling paralysis you cause when you hit, I christen you Lightning Sword Dolphin! Yay! Yes! Yes! Yes!"

"Lightning Sword Dolphin, huh?" Tada pushed up his glasses with his index finger. "That's pretty good."

"I don't think it's good," Shihoru muttered.

"What's not to like?!" Ranta rounded on Shihoru.

"A dolphin's an aquatic mammal, right?" Merry said looking at Ranta with contempt. "No matter how you look at it, it's weird."

"Huh?! Who decided dolphin has to mean an aquatic mammal?!" Ranta shouted "In my head, dolphin's just categorized as a cool word, so Lightning Sword Dolphin is cool! Bam! How do you like that?!"

"Whatever," Haruhiro said. "Let's just go."

"You need to give me more attention, Parupiroooo!"

"Nah, man. I'm boring. I can't."

"Fine, I take it back! You're funny!" Ranta hollered. "Now give me attention! Give me attention, please!"

"You're such a pain," Haruhiro muttered. "'Pay attention to me, pay attention to me'... what, are you in love with me or something, man?"

"Th-there's no way I'd be in love with you, is there?! You moroooon!" Ranta screamed.

"Ahh." Yume smirked. "Your face's gone all red. That's *kiiiinda* suspicious, y'know."

"I'm not turning red! Hold on, my helmet's visor is down! You can't even see my face to tell!"

"Was just sayin' it to get a reaction," smirked Yume. "The way you're protestin', though, that's suspicious, too, huh?"

"...Um." Kuzaku raised his visor and gestured up ahead with his eyes. "Seriously, isn't it time we move on?"

"Heh..." Inui offered his hand to Shihoru. "If you like, how about I escort you?"

"No." Shihoru backed away, shaking her head. "I'm fine, thanks. Besides, you're half-dead, anyway..."

Inui collapsed on the spot, and he didn't try to get back up for a while.

Grimgar of Fantasy and Ash

11. Rondo of the Leopard, Whale, and Dolphin

Tada wasn't complaining, and his expression hadn't changed, but his breathing was ragged. He looked like he was having a hard time.

As for Inui, he was holding onto Shihoru's staff as she used it to pull him along. He'd initially asked her to lend him a shoulder, or to hold his hand, but when Shihoru had curtly refused, he'd begged her to at least let him have this much, and Shihoru had ultimately relented. Even if half of it was an act, Inui was probably suffering, too, somehow.

Kikkawa had apparently busted a few ribs. They seemed to be hurting him sometimes when he moved.

Haruhiro and the others were still wandering through the maze of rubble. They had tried to get back to where they entered, but that only got them more lost.

"If only Anna-san were here..." Kikkawa whined. "Anna-san does, like, make-mapping as a hobby, and because it's useful. It really helps at times like this..."

"With *those* maps...?" Haruhiro couldn't help but ask.

"You just need to know how to read them, man," Kikkawa insisted. "If you know how to read them, you can figure them out. Sure, they're, like, wrong sometimes, but that's all part of the appeal."

"Drop it, Kikkawa," Tada said with a laugh. "We're the only ones who need to understand Anna-san's greatness."

"Yeah, you said it," Ranta snorted, clearly not caring. "You people can keep that stuff to yourselves..."

They were all exhausted. Mentally and physically.

Haruhiro stopped, then looked up at the roof. "...Oh."

"Huh? What is it?" Kuzaku looked up at the ceiling, too.

"Hold on." Haruhiro didn't wait for a response from his comrades before he began scaling the wall of rubble to reach the roof.

He'd called it a roof, but it wasn't like there was a single plate covering the whole thing. There were plenty of gaps. If one was big enough, it wouldn't be impossible to slip through it.

There were lots of bumps and indentations, so the climbing wasn't all that hard. However, it felt like it could come tumbling down easily, so he had to be careful of that.

Sliding his body into a gap, he climbed and climbed. Not looking down as he headed upwards.

He came out.

He was on top of the roof.

It was slanted, so it was a little hard to stand on. While staying crouched, Haruhiro looked around the area.

"We came in from—which way?" he murmured. "Whoa. I'm not sure..."

He had thought if he could get up top, he'd be able to get a handle on their current position, then figure out what direction they should be going to get back, but...now that he'd actually done it, all he'd found was himself standing in the middle of a mountain of rubble.

"No good, huh?" he muttered.

No, but I can't let that get me down, Haruhiro told himself. *It's hardly the first thing that hasn't worked out. Things normally don't work out, and we're always scraping the bottom of the barrel. We've fallen as far as we can fall. It's only up from here.*

"I was being so negative there, it actually ended up swinging back around to being positive..." Haruhiro murmured.

"Haruhiroooo...!" Ranta called out.

"Yeah, yeah..." Haruhiro sighed, then called down to him, "I'm coming back now!"

"You figure anything out?!"

"Yeah, that we're totally lost..." Haruhiro muttered, then went to head back down.

Why had he stopped and decided against it? He wasn't sure. It was just, something bothered him. But what was it...?

Haruhiro stood up. "Oh... Whoa..."

He stumbled a bit, which scared him. He wished he had something to lean on for support. When he looked, not far away, there was a spot that was like a slightly slanted, shallow cup.

In order to get there, he would have to leap over a gap that was easily over a meter wide. Haruhiro hesitated, but he went for it. Well, it wasn't a hard jump by any means. He managed to make it to the cup safely.

What? What was bothering him? Had he heard something? Or, perhaps, seen something?

"Heyyyyyyyyyyyyyyyyyyy! Haruhiro! You ass!" Ranta shouted again.

Haruhiro was about to yell *Shut up!* but then thought better of it. "Ah!" he cried.

They weren't close.

They were far away.

Practically specks off in the distance.

More than a hundred meters away.

He wasn't sure what direction. He'd never been clear on which way was north, south, east, or west here. Anyway, from Haruhiro's perspective, they were ahead of him and to the left. There was rubble piled up there, almost like a tower.

He saw them halfway up. Moving. He couldn't tell what shape they were. But, while the rubble was mostly white, these specks were black.

One, two, three. There were three of them.

Three, Haruhiro told himself.

Tokimune, Anna-san, and Mimorin would make three.

Haruhiro formed his hands into a horn and was about to try calling out to them. He stopped himself just short of doing it.

Bad idea? It might be.

It was probably best to assume there were still more of the cultists and who-knew-what-else inside the maze of rubble. The cultists below might hear Haruhiro's voice.

Haruhiro poked his head through a gap in the roof. "I may have spotted them. Tokimune-san and the others. I can't make them out clearly, though."

"Whaaaaat?!" Ranta screamed.

Now, what were they going to do? Going through the maze of rubble to reach the tower was going to be a lot of work, what with it being a maze and all. On top of that, while the nimble Haruhiro might not have had much trouble getting up here, the heavily armored Kuzaku and Kikkawa would exhaust themselves doing it. Even if everyone managed to get up top, there was still the issue of whether or not they could make it all the way to the tower. There were no paths up here, and it wasn't even level. Still, there was no reason not to try.

The girls came up first, then Inui, Tada, and Kuzaku, with Ranta coming up last. It took some doing, but they managed to get up.

It really did look like there were people in the tower. Yume, with her superb eyesight, said definitively that there were three people there. Distance-wise, it wasn't just a hundred meters away, it was two hundred.

Haruhiro took point, advancing slowly as he searched for pieces of rubble that were viable footholds. Even if it was something of a roundabout route, he prioritized ease of passage while choosing his path. If his comrades couldn't follow him, it would defeat the purpose.

Just to advance ten meters, it was taking five or ten minutes. Haruhiro was mostly fine, but his comrades were getting frustrated. He could understand why. Haruhiro had to focus on choosing a path, and he could focus on that, but the others were just following him. Whenever people had the leeway to do so, they would think about things they probably shouldn't.

Haruhiro stretched out his right foot, testing the rubble. *Will here work? No, it's loose.* He shifted his foot to the left, stepping on a different piece of rubble. *This one seems fine.*

"Ranta," he said.

"Huh? What?"

"What happened to Betrayer?"

"I chucked it," said Ranta. "Who needs that thing? Not me. 'Cause I've got Lightning Sword Dolphin now. If I kept it, it'd just be excess baggage."

"What a waste," Yume complained. Haruhiro couldn't afford to look in Yume's direction right now, but he was sure her cheeks were puffed up.

"Me, I think it's lovely, y'know," said Kikkawa. "The way Ranta does stuff like that. You're the man, Ranta."

"Yeah, you're a guy who gets it, Kikkawa," said Ranta. "I didn't decide you had potential for nothing."

"When did you ever decide he had potential...?" Shihoru muttered.

"Just now?" Ranta shot back.

"In a way, I'm jealous." Merry's voice was so incredibly cold, she didn't sound like she envied him at all.

"I kind of feel that way, too," Kuzaku said in a subdued voice.

"Seriously?" Merry sounded displeased.

"That's Anna-san, all right," Tada suddenly said. "That's Anna-san, Tokimune, and Mimori. No doubt about it. I can tell."

"Yeah..." Inui agreed. "You're right... Heh..."

Hopefully they're right, Haruhiro thought. *But I don't want to get my hopes up prematurely, and I don't want to get emotional and have it disrupt my concentration, so I don't want to think it's them just yet.*

"Haruhiro," Tada called suddenly.

Startled, Haruhiro nearly slipped and fell.

Don't do that! he nearly snapped, but then reconsidered. *Oh, whatever, it's fine.*

"What's up?" he asked.

"You know, you make a surprisingly good leader," said Tada.

"...No, I don't."

"You're as plain as a ladybug, and not as good as Tokimune, though," said Tada.

"I know, right?" Haruhiro said.

He didn't quite know why he'd responded like that. And, wait, what did Tada mean, "plain as a ladybug"? That made no sense. Well, maybe he couldn't expect sense from Tada.

It didn't feel bad being praised, though. It was just, more than anything, it made him feel a bit ticklish, and the strongest feeling he got from it was a desire to say, *Please, stop.*

He wanted to do his best work, to do the best he could for his comrades and those he had ties with. He did have those sorts of feelings, but Haruhiro also really didn't want to stand out. He had finally realized that was the sort of person he was.

What's wrong with being plain? he thought. *Plain is good. Plain is the best. I want to be plain forever.*

Haruhiro wasn't particularly sleepy, but with sleepy eyes, he was searching out a suitable route to the tower, having run-of-the-mill thoughts like, *It's still pretty far,* and, *We're not getting much closer.* But he was a run-of-the-mill sort of guy, after all, so that was no surprise.

However, he didn't stop. He didn't throw in the towel. If he didn't give up, he could move forward one step, or, well, one half-step at a time. Even if he turned back occasionally, he just had to move forward again afterwards. Plainly and boringly, slowly and steadily.

"They're wavin'," Yume said, waving both her arms back at them. "Looks like all three of them are doin' fine."

Haruhiro narrowed his eyes, too, and confirmed that the three who were at the tower were waving their hands. No, only two of them were waving. Tokimune and Anna-san. Mimorin was sitting down and wasn't moving. Tada had said that Mimorin had hurt her leg, or something like that. Hopefully, the injury wasn't too bad. Still, she'd gotten that far, so it couldn't be so bad that she was unable to move.

We're coming now, Haruhiro said silently. *We'll be there in no time. No, it could be a while still, maybe? But, we'll get there eventually. It's just another fifty meters or so, I'd say.*

"Tada! Inui! Kikkawa!" Anna-san called, stretching out with her tiny body. She must have been unable to hold it in any longer.

Tada pressed on his glasses with the index finger of his left hand, then silently lifted his warhammer aloft.

"Heh..." Inui was—tearing up?

Kikkawa looked ready to burst into tears, too, so Ranta slapped him on the shoulder.

"You guys!" Tokimune spread his arms out wide. "Viva Tokkis!"

"What's that he's doing?" Kuzaku whispered.

"A 'T'...?" Merry tilted her head to the side quizzically.

"Oh..." Shihoru didn't sound like she approved. "The 'T' from Tokkis..."

"Hoooh." Yume nodded, seemingly impressed, then looked to Tada. "That's a thing people do, huh? That sort of—what do you call it? Erm, a party pose, kind of thing?"

"No." Tada shook his head. "This is the first time I've seen it."

"Same here..." Inui said. "Heh..."

"It's new to me, too," said Kikkawa. "Oh! It's the 'T' from Tokkis! It's that one, huh?"

What other one did Kikkawa think it might have been? Haruhiro thought. *It doesn't matter which, I guess. Yeah. Whichever it was, it doesn't matter.*

Mimorin really was sitting down. Right now, she just raised her hand a little. She was looking at Haruhiro. They were too far away for him to make out her face, but he could feel her eyes on him.

Haruhiro raised his right hand in response.

Did the usually expressionless Mimorin smile? he thought. *I wonder. Not that it matters. Yeah. It doesn't matter. After all, we'll be there soon anyway.*

Haruhiro tried to step over a largish gap.

"...Whoa," he muttered.

Their eyes met.

It had a lion-like head. White. With one eye. Its body was like a sculpture, but the eyeball was a very eyeball-y eyeball, raw and vivid.

The area beneath the gap was pretty wide, and that thing was looking up at Haruhiro from inside there.

Ah! Aha! So, this is the one I've heard so much about.

"A white gia—"

The white giant reached out towards him. Haruhiro leapt backwards. That thing—it could reach.

"Ohhhhhhhhhhhhhhhhhhh?!" Ranta hollered.

Kikkawa was flipping out, and Haruhiro thought he'd heard the girls scream, too.

The white giant's hand shot out through the gap, and the rubble that made up the ceiling collapsed.

"G-get back! Get back!" Haruhiro shouted commands as he fell back himself.

This is bad, he thought frantically. *Even thinking calmly about it, this is really bad. In order to return along precisely the route we carefully used to come here, it's going to require just as much carefulness on the way back, but now we're in a hurry. More than that, we're panicking.*

"Hyahhhh!" Kikkawa screamed.

Who was that? Kikkawa? Apparently, yes. Kikkawa's gone. He must have fallen through some gap somewhere.

"Meowwwr?!" Yume nearly fell into a hole, too, but clutched onto the rim.

"Heh!" Inui was trying to pull Yume up out of the hole. Ranta, Merry, and Shihoru looked like they meant to help him.

"Dammit! Kikkawa!" Tada slid down through a nearby gap.

"Haruhiro?!" Kuzaku turned to look over in his direction.

Tokimune and the others had also noticed something was amiss, and they were trying to come this way.

This is awful, Haruhiro thought. *An instant. All it took was an instant for everything to go to hell. It's not fair. I was trying my best in my slow and steady, plain and boring way, but this is really awful. It's all a wash. It's just way too awful.*

This is just how things go. I know that. When I pile up the tiny stones of hard work and finally think I have a nice little mountain going, something always comes along and makes it fall apart.

Even so, I won't cry. I'll make an immediate decision. This requires an instantaneous response. If I get it wrong—no, I don't have time to think about what will happen if I get it wrong.

"Ranta, get down there!" Haruhiro shouted. "Inui, you, too! Support Kikkawa and Tada down below! Everyone else, attack it from up here!"

"Man, what do you mean attack—" Ranta began.

"Are you scared, Ranta?!" Haruhiro shouted.

"Don't be stupid! There's no way I'd be scared! Bring it on!" Ranta screamed.

It was a good thing Ranta was an idiot. Inui and Ranta immediately moved into action.

The white giant was using one arm to smash through the rubble like crazy. Attack it from above? Could they really do that?

Yume was already being pulled up. Tokimune and the others would still take time to arrive.

"Don't push yourselves too hard!" Haruhiro shouted to Tokimune, jumping from one piece of rubble to another, heading towards the white giant's back. "Shihoru! Test if Darsh Magic will work or not!"

"Right! Ohm, rel, ect, el, vel, darsh!"

Vwong, vwong, vwong. Three shadow elementals that looked like balls of black seaweed flew towards the white giant.

Shadow Echo. They hit. All three of them. For an instant, it looked like its arm stopped moving, but that was all.

"Maybe not!" Shihoru called.

"Whew!" Yume let an arrow fly, but it bounced off. "No good! It's hard!"

The eye, Haruhiro thought. *That one eye. It seems like a blade would go through there. But the eye, huh? How will I do it?*

"Ohhh!" he cried in realization.

Like this? Is this the only way?

Haruhiro kicked off from the rubble, leaping onto the giant's arm. It really was hard. And cold. Like a boulder. It was impressive that it could move. Haruhiro leapt from the arm to the shoulder. Then to the head.

"That's dangerous, you know?!" he heard Ranta shout.

Yeah, you said it.

Haruhiro circled around to the front of its head, twisting his dagger into its one eye.

Ahh, this looks bad, *he realized.* This thing's definitely gonna thrash around. Should I jump down?

The giant was more than three meters tall. Maybe not four meters, though. It wasn't a height he'd die falling from, but he might get hurt.

While Haruhiro was hesitating, the giant opened its mouth and emitted a rumbling roar. *Go, go, go, go, go...* Then it dove headfirst into the nearby rubble.

Haruhiro circled around to its back side moments before the impact, so he managed to survive somehow. But the giant hadn't stopped yet.

"Go, go, go, go, go, go, go, go, go, go, go, go, go, go, go, go, go...!"

It punched the wall of rubble. It smashed it down. It was all Haruhiro could do to hold on. He had no idea what might happen to him if he was thrown off now.

Actually, does it feel like I'm gonna die even if I do hang on? he thought. *I might. This could be a situation where, if I manage not to die, it would be fair to say I got really lucky.*

"Gwahhhhhhhhh!" Ranta yelled.

Haruhiro thought he caught a glimpse of Ranta rushing towards the giant. A split second later, the giant shuddered slightly and stopped.

It was probably for half an instant, Haruhiro thought. *No, it couldn't be that, could it? Lightning Sword Dolphin. Is that it? Did he slash it with Lightning Sword Dolphin?*

"Ah!" Haruhiro cried.

He threw himself away from the giant's back as hard as he could. When he did, the giant was already starting to move again, and if he missed this chance, he figured he wouldn't get another one.

He had been trying to be careful not to land on anything funny, but his left arm struck something, he hit his tailbone, and his back collided with something hard.

It hurts!...was one thing he couldn't afford to say right now.

The giant was right next to him. Haruhiro rolled away from it. For now, he just needed to put distance between them. It didn't matter how he got it; he just needed that distance.

Once he was further away, and had hidden in the shadow of some of the larger rubble, Haruhiro noticed he couldn't move his left arm.

His butt, he wasn't sure about. It hurt when it touched something. His back hurt, too. Was he bleeding? Apparently. His breathing was fine. Other than his left arm, well, it was just pain. His left arm, though—he wasn't sure. *It might be broken*, he thought.

The giant was rampaging about, seemingly at random.

Where was Ranta? What about Tada? Inui?

At the very least, they didn't seem to be fighting the giant.

"Haru-kuuuun!" He heard Yume's voice from above him.

For just two seconds, he thought about it. Then he called back. "Where are Tokimune-san and his group?!"

"Haru-kun?!" Yume cried. "Er, lessee, they're not here yet!"

"What about the others?!" Haruhiro shouted.

"They're okay!"

"Get away from here!" Haruhiro shouted. "From the giant! We'll join back up later! Ranta! Tada-san, Kikkawa, Inui-san! Can you hear me?!"

"Yeah!" Ranta responded immediately, although Haruhiro couldn't see him.

"Gotcha!" Judging from Kikkawa's voice, he was still full of energy.

"We're getting by somehow!" Tada responded a little after the other two.

There was no response from Inui. Searching for him wasn't an option.

I'm sorry, Inui-san, thought Haruhiro.

"Yume!" he called. "Head towards Tokimune-san and his group, and once you've joined up with them, wait! Ranta! Tada-san, Kikkawa—and Inui-san, too! Find me, and follow me!"

Haruhiro remembered the direction of the tower Tokimune and the others had been in. To go that way, they'd have to rush past the giant, which was dangerous, but they had no choice.

As for his left arm, he could move his shoulder, but nothing past his elbow. It hurt, of course. But not that badly yet. His butt and back were bearable, too.

"Here we go!" Haruhiro shouted, giving the signal to everyone, then took off at a run.

Just to be safe, he chose a time when the giant had its back to him. But as he tried to get past it, the giant made an about-face, which made him panic pretty badly.

Haruhiro couldn't stop or turn back. He had to keep on running past. He nearly got kicked by the giant. Somehow, he managed to dodge its leg and turned back.

Ranta was with him. Kikkawa, too. What about Tada? Or Inui?

"Go, go, go, go, go, go, go, go, go, go, go, go...!" The giant emitted its rumbling roar.

Haruhiro didn't have time to think about it. He needed to worry about himself before others. He'd wounded its one eye, but could it still see? Could it sense him? The giant was chasing after Haruhiro!

"Why?!" Haruhiro screamed.

The giant's movements were languid, but it was twice as big as a human, after all. If it ran straight forward, it would be as fast as a human, maybe faster. Not to mention, Haruhiro was injured. He couldn't run at his top speed.

When Haruhiro leapt behind a wall of rubble, the giant tackled the wall and pulverized it.

"Ow!" Haruhiro shouted.

Pieces of rubble flew everywhere, and Haruhiro ran away while they rained down on him. The giant knocked down piles of rubble, springing into the air in pursuit of Haruhiro.

"I-it looks like...it's holding a grudge?!" he shouted.

"Go, go, go, go, go, go, go, go, go, go, go, go, go, go, go...!"

"O-oh, crap! Th-this is bad!"

Am I gonna die? Haruhiro thought. *Am I really gonna die? Normally, I would, right?*

He wanted to give up.

But Haruhiro was still running towards the tower.

Should I change course? he wondered. *Pull the giant as far away as I can, and then—if I do that, I mean, it might save my comrades.*

Even if he was going to die, he wanted to at least do that much.

That's right. It's not time to die yet. Haruhiro still had things he could do. *I'll pull the giant away from my comrades. It won't be too late to die after that.*

Okay.

With a goal set, he felt the power welling up inside him.

"This way!" he called.

Haruhiro tried to hang a right. That was when it happened.

"Okaaaaaayyyyyyyyyyyyyy!"

What was that? Haruhiro stopped and looked back despite himself.

It looked like the guy had fallen down from up above. In other words, through a gap in the roof. The roof was pretty high around that area, leaving considerable space above the head of the giant, which stood nearly four meters tall. The ceiling was probably around two meters higher than the giant.

The guy had fallen that distance. No, that wasn't it—he had leapt down at the giant from it.

The guy slammed his sword into the giant's head hard. The giant stumbled. It wasn't clear how much damage it had dealt, but it didn't look like the giant could just shrug it off.

Then the guy landed on the giant's shoulders, slugging the side of its big face with his shield.

"Goooooooooooooong!"

The guy used his sword not so much to slash it, as to punch it.

"Daaaaaaaahhhhhhhhh!"

Then, like a deer running through a valley, he stepped lightly from the giant's arms, to its knees, then finally to the ground.

"Wah ha ha! Heeeere's Tokimune-san!" Tokimune banged his sword on his shield loudly. "Bring it on, big guy! I'll make quick work of you!"

"No, that's clearly not going to work, you know?" Haruhiro let his true feelings escape.

"Haruhiro!" Tokimune called.

"Y-yes."

"You're about to witness a miracle! So dig the wax out of your eyes and watch!"

"If I dig out my eyes, I'm not gonna be seeing anything..."

"You're so nitpicky!" Tokimune shouted.

Am I really? Aren't you just too sloppy about things, Tokimune? And random, too. I'm glad you dropped in to help, but this is reckless.

"Go, go, go, go, go, go, go, go, go, go, go, go, go, go, go, go, go...!" The giant crouched down and attacked Tokimune.

Its right fist. It was going to punch. Not straight. A hook.

"Ta-da-da-dahhhh!" Tokimune—wasn't dodging.

No, shouldn't you dodge there? Haruhiro thought.

His shield. Tokimune meant to block the giant's right hook with his shield.

...No. That's not even an option. He's crazy. He's absolutely crazy.

"Guhhhhhhhhhhhhhh...!"

There was an incredible noise, and then Tokimune—was not sent flying. He was holding his ground. He had been pushed back about a meter by the force of the giant's right hook, but he'd stopped there.

"Yay! Ta-da!" Tokimune shouted.

Before the giant could pull back its right arm, incredibly, Tokimune raced up it. Where had he gotten that sense of balance? How could he commit like that?

Tokimune reached the giant's right shoulder in no time. Then, once again, he smacked the giant in the side of its face with his sword

and shield.

"Gooooooooong! Daaaaahhhhhhhhhh!"

The giant staggered a little, but soon tried to catch Tokimune with its hands. Only, it was slow and stupid. Tokimune jumped away, pulling off a stylish landing, then whaled on the giant's knees with his sword.

"Take that! And that! And that! And that! And that! And that, and that, and that, and that!"

"Go, go, go, go, go, go...!"

The giant swung down its right arm, trying to crush Tokimune. It was a terrifying strike that threatened to make an instant pancake out of him, but Tokimune dodged it with a laugh. Using a back flip, for some reason.

"That was unnecessary," Haruhiro commented.

"It was *too* necessary!" Tokimune shouted. He got in close to the giant, visiting blows on it with his sword and shield. "Because it was damn cool! Strong and cool are synonymous—yeahhhhhh!"

"Tch! Dammit, Tokimune!" a man shouted.

It was Tada. Tada was here. He was bleeding all over, but Tada ran forward with his warhammer over his shoulder.

"I don't care who's cooler, but I'm stronger!" Tada bellowed. "Somersault Bomb!"

That skill—he ran up, did a forward somersault, then slammed his weapon down into the enemy. That wasn't a priest's self-defense skill. A warrior. It was a warrior's heavy armor combat skill.

Ker-smash! Tada's warhammer caught the giant's left knee. The giant's knee caved in, causing white fragments to fly everywhere.

Tada did a backwards roll to get behind it, then was unable to get up, lying on his backside. "Urgh... Not enough blood..."

"Wah ha ha! It's 'cause you're trying too hard, Tada! Whoa there..." Tokimune slipped through the giant's arms as he fell back, then hit those arms with his sword. He hit them and hit them. "But that was a good attack there! It's slowed it down!"

It was true, the giant was dragging its left leg. Tada's Somersault Bomb must have been pretty effective.

"Seriously?! Are we seriously, seriously going to finish this thing here?!" a voice screamed.

Someone annoying had arrived. It was Ranta.

"Then that's gotta mean, gotta mean, gotta mean it's my time to shine, right?!" Ranta hollered.

No, you get lost! was what Haruhiro wanted to say, but Ranta wouldn't have listened.

"Yahoo!" Kikkawa yelled. "I'm getting in on this too!"

"Haru!" Merry called.

"Haru-kun!" cried Yume.

"Haruhiro-kun..." murmured Shihoru.

"Haruhiro?!" cried Kuzaku.

Yeah, and it looks like everyone's come down here now, Haruhiro noted. *We're doing this. Is that the way things are going? It probably is. I don't like it. I mean, my left arm, butt, and back hurt. If we're going to do this, we have to win. Sure, it's slowed down a bit, but can we take down that monster?*

Haruhiro didn't think it was going to be that easy.

The giant was going after Tokimune, reaching out with its right hand, then its left. Tokimune was nimbly avoiding its grasp and striking back, but he wasn't managing to do any damage.

Tada was still on the ground. It didn't look like he'd be able to move. Ranta and Kikkawa seemed to be trying to get behind the giant. Yume, Shihoru, Merry, and Kuzaku were trying to get closer to Haruhiro.

Haruhiro's left arm was starting to seriously hurt now. It kept drawing his attention, and he couldn't help it. He needed to get his mind back on track. What was it? What did he need to be thinking about? Reinforcements. That was right. Enemies. There could be cultists coming. There didn't seem to be any yet.

They had to take it down. Kill it. That giant. How? Tada's warhammer. The giant's...outer skin? Was it skin? He wasn't sure, but the giant's outside was really hard. It seemed bludgeoning weapons would still work, though. Even so, it was too much to ask Tada to pull off another hit like before. Haruhiro's sap was a bludgeoning weapon, too, but he'd be hard-pressed to pull off a powerful attack like Tada had with it. Or rather, it would be impossible to. Merry's short staff was probably a similar case. That left magic, maybe. The cultists had been weak against Darsh Magic. What about the giant?

Shadow Bond couldn't bind powerful enemies to begin with, so it was going to be pointless. Even if Shadow Complex could confuse the giant, if it thrashed around violently, it wouldn't be any different. That one was out, too.

What about putting it to sleep with Sleepy Shadow? It would wake up if they attacked it, so that one was also no good. Shadow Echo didn't seem like it would be a game-changer, either.

"What do we do?" Haruhiro mumbled to himself as he looked around them, and above.

Where are Anna-san and Mimori? he wondered. Had Inui not

managed to keep up with the group, after all? What was he going to do?

"Kuzaku, you join in and help surround it," Haruhiro said. "Don't get too close. Yume and Merry, cover Shihoru. Shihoru, use magic. Try nailing it with a Thunderstorm."

"Right!" Shihoru immediately turned to face the giant. "Everyone, get back a little!"

Tokimune and the others backed away from the giant. Shihoru began to draw elemental sigils with the tip of her staff and chant a spell.

"Jess, yeen, sark, kart, fram, dart!"

It was a big target, so the entire bundle of lightning struck the giant. There was a pretty incredible noise, and the giant's body shook, with smoke rising from it here and there, but, as if everything were normal, it turned to look in their direction—or rather, in Shihoru's direction.

Oh, crap, Haruhiro thought. *Here it comes.*

"I'm not gonna let you—" Ranta stabbed Lightning Sword Dolphin into the giant. "—Do thaaaat!"

The giant shuddered. That was all. Then it reached out and tried to grab Ranta. "Go, go, go...!"

"Whoa, hoh!" Ranta let out a weird cry and swung Lightning Sword Dolphin again. The tip of the blade grazed the middle finger of the giant's right hand.

The giant shuddered.

Ranta leapt back during that time, and Tokimune and Kikkawa, along with Kuzaku, closed in on the giant, whaling on its lower extremities with their swords and shields. However, no matter how much they hit it, they couldn't do the same kind of damage that Tada's Somersault Bomb had.

"Go, go, go, go, go, go...!"

"Whoa!" Tokimune shouted.

"Yipes!" Kikkawa screamed.

"Wha...!" Kuzaku cried.

When the giant made a grand swing with both of its arms, Tokimune, Kikkawa, and Kuzaku were all forced to back away. Could they really defeat it by just repeatedly doing this?

"Haruhiro!" Tokimune shouted to him while dodging the giant's right hook. "As your senior, let me teach you the secret to beating down enemies like this!"

"What's that secret?!" Haruhiro shouted back.

"A concentrated attack!"

"Come again?"

"You concentrate your attacks! If there're five people, that's five times the attacks! If you have ten people, it's ten! You slam all of that into it at once! A focused attack! That's the secret!"

"...I see," Haruhiro muttered. He felt like an idiot to have expected anything.

What's the big deal about a concentrated attack? You're just concentrating your attacks. Anyone would think to do that. It's obvious, isn't it?

The issue was *where* to concentrate their attacks. *How* would they concentrate their attacks?

A concentrated attack, Haruhiro thought.

"Mimorin! Keep trying, yeah!" a new voice shouted.

That voice, that way of talking—*it's Anna-san,* he realized.

Looking up, he saw Mimorin wedged into a gap in the ceiling. No, she wasn't wedged in there; she was trying to come down. Her chest was kind of large, though, and she seemed to have gotten stuck. Still, she slipped through.

Or rather, she fell.

"Eek!" Mimorin landed on her rump, letting out a surprisingly cute little scream as she did. Then she groaned. "Ngh..."

The fall looked like it had been painful.

"Mi-Mi-Mimoriiiin?!" Anna-san was trying to come down through the same gap. She had large breasts, too, but unlike Mimori, her body was small, so it didn't look like she'd get caught. "*Are you all right?!* You not hurt, yeah?!"

"It's nothing major." Mimorin used her staff for support as she got up, then drew her sword.

That's right, Haruhiro remembered.

She was a mage now, but Mimorin had once been a warrior, and she also carried a sword in addition to her staff. What was Mimorin planning to do with her staff in her left hand and her sword in her right?

For now, she looked around restlessly, then seemed to find what she was after. She started walking towards it, but her leg was injured, and it looked like her butt hurt, too, so she was tottering unsteadily.

"Hold on, that's dangerous," Haruhiro told her.

Mimorin was trying to face down the giant. She was apparently going to join in on the concentrated attack. Why did everyone in the Tokkis have to be like this?

Concentrating our attacks, Haruhiro thought.

No plan came to mind. Fighting this way was absurd. Why did

they even need to defeat the giant to begin with? Dealing a major blow to it, to buy the time to retreat, would be enough. Any more was unnecessary.

"Ranta!" Haruhiro shouted. "Keep on whacking the giant's legs with that Lightning Sword you're so proud of! When you do, everyone will go for the eye! It can still see with that eye! We'll blind it, then run! You can complain later, just do what I say for now! Now, do it, Ranta!"

"Don't act so full of yourself when you're just Parupiro!" Ranta hollered. He closed in on the giant and hit its leg with Lightning Sword Dolphin. "You'd better cry and thank me later!"

Not gonna happen, Haruhiro thought. *I'll never thank you, but if you do well, I might praise you for it.*

"Hah! Hah! Hah! Hah! Hah! Hah! Hah! Hahhhhh...!" Ranta swung Lightning Sword Dolphin continuously, without stopping for a breath. He swung it like crazy, striking the giant's left leg.

Each time he hit the giant, it shuddered. Shudder, shudder, shudder, shudder. Each of those shudders only took a short time, but when they came continuously, it was almost like it was paralyzed, because the giant couldn't move.

"Mrrow!" Yume nocked an arrow to her composite bow, then let it loose.

In rapid succession, she fired, and fired, and fired, and fired.

It was the archery skill, Rapid Fire. With Yume's skill level, every couple shots one would fire off in completely the wrong direction, or not fly far enough, but two in every five hit the giant right in the eye. This was a result so successful, Haruhiro could only imagine it was a fluke.

"Haruhiroooo!" Tokimune raced up the giant's body. "It looks like you've mastered the secret! Now it's time for my super attack! Float like a leopard, sting like a whale!"

You've got something wrong there, Haruhiro thought. *You probably meant "float like a butterfly, sting like a bee."*

But it would be uncouth to correct him—maybe? Besides, Tokimune didn't float like a butterfly or a leopard, and he didn't sting like a whale or a bee. However, once he got up on the giant's shoulders, he did stab the hell out of its one eye.

"Me, too! Me, too! Let me in on this!" Kikkawa tried to climb the giant, too, but failed.

Kuzaku shook his head, as if to say, *Yeah, no, I can't.* Haruhiro was more or less fine with that. He was the one who'd said everyone should attack its eye, but maybe Tokimune alone would be enough.

Of course, Mimorin, who was injured, didn't need to do anything. Haruhiro rushed over to Mimorin, patting her on the back lightly.

"You've done enough! Let's run, Mimorin!"

"Huh?" Mimorin looked down at Haruhiro, then nodded. "Okay."

Haruhiro waved his right arm wide, calling out loudly, "Retreat! We're retreating! Tokimune-san, get down here! Kikkawa, you, too!"

"Zwahhhhhhhhhhhhhh!" Tada, who had been hanging his head until this point, shouted as he rushed towards the giant.

Before Haruhiro could say, *No, we've done enough,* and stop him, Tada did a forward somersault and slammed his warhammer into the giant's right knee.

"Somersault Booooomb!"

Crunch. The giant's right knee caved in.

Tada stumbled backwards, then sat down. "How do you like that?

I'm the strong one here... heh heh..."

Who really cares? Haruhiro thought.

"Nwahhhh!" Ranta backed away two, three steps, then thrust Lightning Sword Dolphin into the ground. "I-I'm... so... exhausted... dammiiiiit!"

This is the limit, huh? Haruhiro thought.

The giant began to move.

Ultimately, Kikkawa, who had never fully managed to scale the giant, came down from it, half falling off in the process, and helped Tada to his feet. He lent him a shoulder for support, and made him walk.

"Tadacchi! You can go, right?!" Kikkawa called.

"Damn straight!" Tada called. "Who do you think I am?!"

Tokimune made a graceful landing. "Anna-saaaan! We're getting out of here! You know the way, right?!"

"Of course, yeah?!" Anna-san was still clinging to the wall of rubble, but she nimbly jumped down. "You follow Anna-san, yeah! *Let's go!*"

Was this going to be okay? Haruhiro wasn't fully convinced, but he didn't know the way himself, so he had no choice but to let Anna-san lead on.

"Ranta-kun!" Kuzaku dragged Ranta behind him.

"Go, go, go, go, go, go, go, go, go, go, go, go, go, go, go...!"

The giant might have been trying to thrash about, but with both legs collapsing underneath it, it was forced to squat. The two Somersault Bombs had hurt its knees badly.

Haruhiro looked quickly to Yume, Shihoru, and Merry. "Follow Anna-san!" he shouted.

All three nodded in unison.

Anna-san and Tokimune took the lead; then Yume, Shihoru, and Merry; Kuzaku and Ranta followed, as well as Kikkawa and Tada; and lastly, Haruhiro and Mimorin followed them, in that order. They were far from running away at top speed. Even setting Ranta aside, Tada and Mimorin were in no shape to run. The best they could manage would be a hurried walk.

Mimorin had returned her sword to its sheath and was using her staff like a cane, but she was still having a hard time. It looked like she'd lost the strength in her left leg. She was bleeding, too.

If her left side was weak, if he supported her left side with his right, she might have an easier time of it. Fortunately, it was Haruhiro's left arm that hurt. If it had been his right, it would have made things difficult, but this he could handle.

Haruhiro smoothly slid in between Mimorin's left arm and her left flank, putting his right arm around her shoulder.

"Let's do our best," he tried saying to her, but Mimorin didn't say a thing. When he looked, she was biting her lip. It looked like she might burst into tears at any second.

The giant was behind them, putting a great deal of effort into tackling the walls of rubble, grabbing onto chunks of rubble and throwing them. Hopefully, none of it would fly their way.

This is kinda awkward, thought Haruhiro.

They had been working with the Tokkis to explore the Dusk Realm, which they had both discovered, after all, and—well, the Tokkis had stabbed them in the back and tried to steal a march on Haruhiro and the party, but they still felt like comrades, and that was why the party had accepted Kikkawa's request and come this far.

Having come all this way, Haruhiro wanted to save anyone he could, and that was a feeling that didn't apply to any particular individual, but to the Tokkis as a whole. Of course, that whole included Mimorin. That was all there was to it. What he was doing now was just another part of that. He could explain he didn't mean anything else by it, and maybe he should have, but this really wasn't the time, was it?

"Um... say, Mimorin," said Haruhiro. "Uh... I-Inui-san's kind of not here, you know. Nobody's saying anything, though."

"Ohh," said Mimorin.

"Is that okay?" Haruhiro asked. "No, I mean, there's no way it's okay, but..."

"It's okay."

"Huh?"

"I think."

"Y-you think?"

"He's a stubborn survivor, that Inui." Mimorin was back to her usual deadpan expression. "Like a cockroach."

"...Wow," Haruhiro murmured.

"But he's not cute like a cockroach."

No—I'm pretty sure cockroaches aren't cute.

But, even if he said something normal like that, Mimorin probably wouldn't be able to understand. He had a feeling that this girl and he would never understand one another. They didn't have to, though. He didn't particularly want to understand her.

I don't care, he told himself. *It doesn't matter.*

First, they had to get out of the maze of rubble. Then, they could get out of the Dusk Realm. Once they were able to receive the blessings of the God of Light, Lumiaris, they'd heal up with light magic. Then they would return to the Lonesome Field Outpost.

I don't care what happens after that, Haruhiro added silently.

"*My God!*" exclaimed Anna-san, coming to a stop in the middle of a four-way intersection.

Everyone had to stop.

"Hey, hey, hey, hey, Anna-san!" Ranta sputtered.

"*Shut the fuck up!*" Anna-san turned around and said something foreign that probably meant she wanted him to shut up. "*'Kay!* We going, yeah! I make *little bit* mistake! No big deal, yeah!"

"Is that actually true?" Kuzaku mumbled to himself.

"You people." Tokimune gave them the thumbs up and flashed his white teeth at them. "Come on, just trust Anna-san. I'm sure we're about to witness a miracle. Yes, a miracle. No doubt about it."

Tokimune was a big fan of miracles, apparently. Haruhiro couldn't help but want to simply retort, *They're called miracles because they don't usually happen,* but he refrained. That was primarily because he had bigger concerns.

Straight ahead of them, across the four-way intersection, a whole bunch of cultists appeared.

To the right, too.

And on the left, as well.

"Which way is it, Anna-san?!" Tokimune shouted.

Anna-san pointed to the path to the left. "That way, yeah! *Maybe... Absolutely!* Absolutely that way, yeah?!"

"No, asking us won't help," Haruhiro couldn't help but point out.

Anna-san glared at him.

"One, two, three, four..." Tokimune was getting a rough count of the number of incoming cultists. "Well, it'd be tough to run away. We'll have to kill them, huh?"

Haruhiro didn't bother counting. But, well, they were going to have to kill them. That was a fact.

Haruhiro moved away from Mimorin and tried moving his left arm. It hurt. It hurt intensely. It didn't even move all that well. He drew his dagger with his right hand. The number of cultists was five in front, five more to the right, and four to the left. That was a lot. There might be more coming, too.

"Ohm, rel, ect, el, krom, darsh!" Shihoru drew elemental sigils with her staff and chanted the spell for Shadow Mist. The black mist-like shadow elemental burst forth, drifting towards the cultists down the right-hand path.

This'll work—or it should, Haruhiro thought. *It's there. How is it?*

The five cultists all collapsed.

Follow up with another one down the left-hand path or straight ahead, was what he would have liked to tell Shihoru to do, but it wasn't an option. The cultists were already too close, and some of the party would end up in the area of effect, too.

"Man, Haruhiro! I sure am glad you guys came along!" Tokimune yelled.

Tokimune took off. Straight ahead. Knocking aside a cultist's outstretched spear with his shield, he aimed for the eye. The cultist leaned back to avoid it, but Tokimune kept charging forward. He pushed down that cultist, then used Bash on the cultist to his left. At the same time, he used his sword to knock away the cultist on his right.

"We owe you for life, man!" Kikkawa shouted. "I love you, Harucchi!"

Kikkawa followed after Tokimune. It seemed Tokimune acted like no paladin should, rushing in and messing up the enemy, while Kikkawa would go in and attack the enemy Tokimune had left in utter disarray, while taking their attacks and serving as a tank.

"I'm on break," or so Tada said, as he nonetheless sent a cultist flying with a shower of blows from his warhammer.

Mimorin used a two-handed staff and sword style, standing in front of Anna-san.

"Do it! *Kill them all!* Massacre, yeah!" Anna-san was apparently the team's designated cheerleader.

"Ahh, this is dangerous!" Kuzaku cried.

Even as he complained, Kuzaku charged into the left cultists' line of spears. While he did have a sturdy shield, it was obviously still scary. But, despite what Kuzaku said, he didn't falter. Even as the spears scratched his shield, he closed in on a cultist and swung around his longsword. He thrust. The four cultists stopped advancing.

"Don't worry!" Ranta declared, attacking the four cultists whose momentum Kuzaku had killed. "I'm here! Here I go! Secret skill... Dolphin Dance!"

For a moment, the vivid image of a pod of dolphins jumping around playfully flashed through Haruhiro's mind.

Dolphins. They were sea creatures. Since coming to Grimgar, Haruhiro hadn't been to the sea even once. Despite that, he knew what the sea was, and he could imagine it. He knew what dolphins were, too. Had Haruhiro seen dolphins at the sea before?

Regardless, this had basically nothing to do with dolphins.

Ranta slapped the cultists' spears with Lightning Sword Dolphin. When he did, the cultists' bodies shuddered. Using that gap, Ranta stepped in and hit their bodies with Lightning Sword Dolphin. Because of those coats they wore, he couldn't cut them, but the cultists convulsed and collapsed. Kuzaku pressed the attack. Ranta took full advantage of the situation to attack, too.

"Use Stop-eye, then...Quick-eye!" Yume nocked an arrow to her composite bow, moving her eyes around and squinting them.

These were archery skills. Stop-eye used special eye exercises, methods of breathing, and methods regulating the body to increase shooting accuracy. Quick-eye was something like a trick for hitting moving targets.

She fired.

One cultist took an arrow in the eye.

"Nice, Yume!" Haruhiro praised her as he headed for the collapsed cultists down the right-hand path. "Merry, take care of Shihoru!"

"Okay, leave it to me!" Merry called.

Even with his left arm out of commission, Haruhiro could still handle this much. Or rather, he had to handle it. He was going to finish off the cultists Shihoru had put to sleep.

His dagger gouged out each of the cultists' one eye. He did nothing unnecessary. He just jabbed his dagger, held with a backhand grip, deep into their one eye, twisted, and tore it free. Haruhiro probably had sleepy eyes right now. He didn't feel anything. He carried it out like routine work.

Three down, two to go.

Cultists were rushing in his direction from further down the path. Or rather, they'd come around a corner right next to him, so the danger was already close at hand. Yes, *they*. Sadly, it was more than one. Two. No, three.

Reinforcements. He had considered the possibility. He hadn't done anything to prepare for it. There was nothing he could have done. The party's hands had been full enough as it was.

I guess it can't go that easily, huh? Haruhiro thought.

"Haru?!" Merry shouted.

It looked like she had noticed the difficult situation Haruhiro had fallen into. That might mean magical help from Shihoru would be coming. Would she make it in time? Who knew. It could go either way. After all, Haruhiro was already trying to Swat the leading cultist's spear with his dagger. He knocked it aside, somehow.

The spears were coming. One after another.

It's not looking like I can do this, you know? he thought.

While he focused his nerves on using Swat to deflect the cultists' spears, Haruhiro prepared himself for the worst.

Rather than resign myself to it, I need to think about what to do next. Of course, I don't have the time to. Still, I need to think about it and give orders. I may not be much of one, but I am the leader, after all. No, maybe I really can't do this...?

He failed at using Swat. That was because he was thinking about things he shouldn't be.

On his right arm, the cultist's spear sliced off the flesh between his wrist and his elbow. He nearly dropped his dagger.

With the dagger in his weakened right hand, he tried to Swat the next spear. Somehow, he managed it. But the next one was going to be pretty hard. Well, it was probably impossible. Even so, he couldn't stand to just die quietly.

Haruhiro tried to Swat. He missed.

"Heh!" Inui called.

Someone had beaten him to the punch. Behind the cultist who was trying to skewer Haruhiro, a man wearing an eyepatch appeared. With his trademark—or maybe it wasn't, Haruhiro didn't know—ponytail having come undone, his hair was loose and disheveled. But, still, it was Inui.

Inui caught the cultist's head between his hands, then twisted hard, and suddenly...

You know, I think I've seen it somewhere before, Haruhiro thought. *That killing style.*

Inui had probably broken the cultist's neck. It wasn't clear if the cultist had died instantly, but it slumped to the ground limply.

The remaining two must have been surprised, because they turned to look at Inui. By that point, Inui had already drawn his two swords.

Inui stabbed his sword through one cultist's eye. The other cultist twisted his neck, evading Inui's sword.

His back, Haruhiro thought.

The cultist's back was half-turned to Haruhiro. When that happened, sometimes he would see it. That line.

Haruhiro practically glued himself to the cultist's back, kicking his heel into the back of the cultist's knee to break his stance. His left arm wouldn't move properly. However, it wasn't completely immobile. He put his left elbow against the cultist's neck, then put his body weight on it. At the same time, he mustered what strength he had remaining to ram his dagger through the cultist's one eye. The cultist jerked a couple of times, his body convulsing.

Is he dead?

Yeah, he was dead.

Haruhiro couldn't hold the dagger any longer, and he let go of it.

The cultist slumped to the ground.

"Ow..." Haruhiro mumbled. He was ready to cry. At this point, his right hand was more or less useless.

"Heh..." Inui picked up the dagger, then held it up in front of Haruhiro's nose. "In the end, was it over so easily for you?"

No, you don't know that, Haruhiro thought. *What's that line supposed to mean? Are you an idiot? And, wait, why are you alive? Damn, you're stubborn. Seriously, you're like a cockroach. What's with you?*

"I thought you were dead." Haruhiro forced himself to accept the dagger using his right hand, which was causing him a distressing amount of pain. He couldn't feel his fingertips. "I'm glad I was wrong."

"I call myself Inui the Immortal!"

"It's just a self-proclaimed title, huh?"

"At last, it seems the time has come for me to unleash my true power!" Inui added.

"And you're not even listening to what I say..."

"Heh..." Inui took off his eyepatch and threw it away. "Now, I begin in earnest."

His left eye was...normal.

He hadn't been left with one eye after some injury? Well, what was the eyepatch for, then?

"Follow me, Harunire!" Inui cried.

Inui looked like he was about to walk off, but then he stopped to stab two cultists to death, the ones Shihoru had put to sleep, who'd been looking like they were on the verge of waking up.

I don't really understand him, but he seems reliable, Haruhiro thought.

"I'm not Harunire, though. I'm Haruhiro," he said.

Tokimune and his group pushed, and pushed, and pushed like crazy, trying to wipe out the five remaining cultists. Ranta's group had taken down two of their four. Inui moved soundlessly, not towards Tokimune's group, but to Ranta's. Then, without missing a beat in between the two, he buried his swords in the two cultists' single eyes.

"Huh...?" Kuzaku said.

"Hey!" Ranta yelled. What do you think you're—wait, Inui?!"

Kuzaku and Ranta were dumbstruck.

"Pissants..." Inui pulled his swords free from the cultists, then turned slowly with a devilish smile on that face of his, which looked middle-aged. "Prostrate yourselves before my true power. For I am Inui! The Demon Lord, Inui!"

"Not again, yeah." Anna-san slapped her own forehead. "Well, fine. Everyone, follow Demon Lord Inui, yeah! Demon Lord Inui! *Go!*"

"Ha ha ha!" Tokimune kicked the last cultist to the ground, stabbing his sword into his one eye. "Hey, Inui! You were alive! And you're in *that* mode, too, huh! We'll just have to roll with it! Haruhiro, let Inui do as he pleases! When he gets like this, there's no stopping him anyway!"

It's not just Inui, Haruhiro thought exhaustedly. *All of you people basically do whatever you want, and you can't be stopped.*

Inui was charging down the stone path at a good clip.

Haruhiro groaned. "Let's follow him."

Oh, whatever, thought Haruhiro. *Let whatever happens happen. Or rather, I'm sure it'll all work out.*

If it all went south, they could use the Tokkis as disposable pawns and escape. Even if they did, his conscience probably wouldn't fault him for it. No, not probably—it definitely wouldn't. The Tokkis would have no right to hold it against them. Haruhiro and the party had done enough. No, they had done more than enough. To the point they had done more than they should have.

In the time between then until they left the maze of rubble, Haruhiro lost count of how many cultists they took out. However, with his eyepatch off, Inui was ridiculously strong. Tokimune was getting into a good groove, too. Kikkawa was in high spirits. Tada looked intense. Ranta was loud and annoying. Kuzaku was trying hard. Anna-san lost the path multiple times. Yume, Merry, and Shihoru took turns supporting Haruhiro and Mimorin.

Finally, when they escaped the maze of rubble, Inui suddenly collapsed. On closer inspection, it wasn't just that his hair was disheveled; he had wounds all over his body. He was so heavily injured, it was a wonder that he'd been moving around like he was totally fine. When Merry, Anna-san, and Yume tried to care for him, Inui didn't even move, but when Shihoru reluctantly talked to him, he suddenly sat up. That said, he was having a hard time walking, and that was true for Tada, Mimorin, and Haruhiro, too.

Whether they were having a hard time of it or not, they had to walk back towards that initial hill.

Twice, maybe three times, Haruhiro saw Manato and Moguzo off in the distance.

That girl who was facing in his direction, was she Choco, maybe?

The next thing he knew, Tokimune and the others were trying to chase off a one-eyed dog.

Leave it alone, Haruhiro recalled saying. Though, he might not actually have said it. It might not have been Haruhiro. Someone else might have said it.

"Ohh! Look!" Ranta yelled in a big loud voice like an idiot.

He was an idiot, though. Haruhiro looked idly for Ranta. Ranta was right next to him. He was pointing at something. Haruhiro looked in that direction.

"That's bad news..." Kuzaku, or someone else muttered.

"Sure is," someone, maybe Tokimune, replied with a laugh.

It was a silhouette the size of a mountain.

The giant they had fought in the maze of rubble had been four meters tall, at most. They had seen a giant before on the Quickwind Plains, too. That one had surprised him, too, but it paled in comparison to this. It was a few hundred meters away, but it was truly as big as a mountain.

That giant was moving around, slowly.

It was walking.

Who said, "Someday, I'm gonna beat that thing down"? It might have been Tada, Haruhiro thought.

It was impossible.

Wait, why would you want to beat it? Haruhiro thought. He didn't understand. Haruhiro didn't understand it at all. He didn't know when he'd started walking again, either.

Even when they were attacked by the cultists hiding in the shadows of the pillar rocks, and Merry was forced to swing around her short staff, all Haruhiro could do was crawl around and try to get away.

After a while, he lost consciousness. Whenever he came to, he was always being lent a shoulder by someone, and was surprised to find himself walking on his own feet.

He was in pain, yes, but he didn't have a leg injury like Mimori, so he figured he was better off.

At some point, a cloth was wrapped around the wound on his right arm, and that cloth was dark, red, and wet. Who'd wrapped it for him?

The wound on his back might be a surprisingly tricky one. He couldn't feel anything from his back to his waist, but it felt strangely heavy.

"Don't die, man," Ranta said with a serious look on his face.

Was that a dream? Or was it reality?

"Like I could die and leave you behind..." Haruhiro mumbled.

That's what he responded, but, I'm saying something weird, he thought. *No. It was a mistake. Why would I have to die before Ranta? Don't be silly. If you look at the way both of us act on a day-to-day basis, Ranta's gotta die before me. I'm not gonna let myself die before Ranta, damn it.*

That was what he'd wanted to say.

When that initial hill came into sight, Kikkawa carried him.

It's fine, no need to do so much for me, Haruhiro thought, but he lacked the strength to speak up and refuse.

When they entered the hole, and advanced down it a ways, it seemed the blessing of Lumiaris had returned. Merry cast Sacrament on Haruhiro. The effect was immediate. He still felt groggy, but the pain vanished completely. His head cleared, and he at last met with the goddess called relief.

"Everyone's okay...huh?" Haruhiro mumbled.

The Tokkis had two priests, Anna-san and Tada. The two of them had, incredibly, not learned Sacrament yet, but with Merry helping, too, the healing was done in no time.

"That was an incredible experience." Sitting with his back leaning against the rock wall, Kuzaku let out a deep sigh. "No, maybe not so much incredible as terrible, I guess..."

"Honestly..." Merry was crouched next to Kuzaku. "I've had enough..."

"That's right." Yume was letting the lantern she was holding bob around for no reason. She looked sleepy. "For stuff like this, y'know, doin' it maybe once a year is enough."

"I don't think I want it even once a year..." Shihoru looked exhausted, too.

"Weaklings." Tada used the index finger of his left hand to adjust his glasses. "You're all weak. This is why you never move up in the world. Try to learn from our example."

"Hell no," Haruhiro said firmly.

"Huh?" Tada clicked his tongue, looking down at Haruhiro diagonally. "Well, this time, since you were able to bask in the honor of helping us, you must have felt a lot of things, too. Ruminate on this experience, and grow from it. If you don't, it won't have been worth letting you help us."

"Um, Tada-san, why are you being so condescending?" Haruhiro asked.

"Because I'm better than you, duh."

"...Are you now?" Haruhiro asked.

"What, Haruhiro?" Tada snapped. "Do you think you're better than me?"

"No... Rather, I don't really care who's better than who," Haruhiro said.

"Ha ha ha ha," Kikkawa laughed. "That's so you, Harucchi. I kind of love that side of you, you know?"

"...Sure," Haruhiro said. "I kind of envy how you can take things so lightly."

"Yahoo! I got envied! Yay, yay! Hey, hey, Anna-san, Anna-san, did you hear that? Did you hear? I've got someone who envies me. For my...superiority? Rarity? Incomparable lightness! I am super light!"

"Kikkawa, you not *light*, you *shallow*!" Anna-san called. "Yeah?!"

"Huh? What? What? I don't know what *shallow* means, whatever shallow I do?! Just kidding!"

"Not funny! You want to die?! *Shallow* mean frivolous! Yeah!"

"Wow. Frivolous, huh. That one, huh?! Frivolous! It sounds kinda luxurious to me?! Is my value on a sudden rise?! Or, like, am I priceless?!"

"Kikkawa's value is *forever zero,* yeah?!" Anna-san yelled.

"Whaa?! Like, multiply it or divide it, it's still zero?! It'll never change, you mean?! Whoa, Anna-san, I didn't know you thought so much of me! I'd never have thought it! I'm so happy?! There's, like, tears in my eyes?!"

It was odd to say it now, since this happened every time, but Kikkawa's positivity was so out there that it was like a supernatural phenomenon. Haruhiro didn't just find it surprising or appalling. He found it scary.

It is scary. It really is, he thought. *There's something wrong with him. How can he be so cheerful and energetic, even after what we went through?*

"Heh..." Inui walked along while swaying, then stopped in front of Shihoru. He had thrown his eyepatch away, so he no longer had it, but his left eye was closed. He might have been sealing away his true power. The man was an idiot.

"Allow me to give you one very important right," Inui said. "The right to be my wife, that is... Heh..."

"I-I don't want that." Shihoru stuttered, but she replied immediately.

"I don't hate reserved girls," Inui said.

"I, um... I don't like people like you, so..."

"You don't...like me?" Inui asked.

"...Right."

"You don't hate me, either?"

"I-I wouldn't say I hate you..." Shihoru said.

"You neither like nor hate me... then."

"W-well... Yeah... That's right."

"Very well." Inui turned on his heel. "In time, you, too, will come to understand...the hidden truth, that is... Heh..."

"I don't want to understand, though," Shihoru said.

"Kwah ha ha... Heh heh heh... Ha ha ha ha ha!" Laughing as he went, Inui departed for the Dusk Realm.

"Huh?" Haruhiro looked to each of the Tokkis. "Y-you're okay with this? Huh? Inui-san's going by himself..."

"It fine, yeah." Anna-san waved her hand and laughed. "He have *broken heart*? He in shock, so better leave him alone, yeah."

"But, isn't it dangerous?" Haruhiro asked.

"Well, he probably won't die!" Tokimune laughed as he walked up, giving them a peek at his white teeth as he extended his right hand to Haruhiro. "That aside, thanks, Haruhiro!"

"...Nah." Haruhiro hesitantly took Tokimune's hand. "Well, it's a bit awkward after you guys tried to steal a march on us."

"Aha ha! Don't let that bother you!" Tokimune called.

"I've kind of realized that letting it bother me wouldn't do any good..."

"There you have it! We didn't mean any harm! Forgive us!"

"Couldn't you at least apologize first?" Haruhiro asked.

"Man." Tokimune stopped shaking Haruhiro's hand and playfully slapped him on the cheeks. "You act like you're weak, but you can speak your mind pretty well, huh?"

"S-stop it," Haruhiro said. "Don't touch me like that."

"When you tell me to stop, it makes me want to stop less, you know?" Tokimune asked.

"Th-then don't stop!"

"Gotcha. I won't stop."

"Whaa..." Haruhiro muttered.

"What do you mean, 'Whaa'? Don't make me kiss you."

"No, seriously, don't do that!" Haruhiro yelled.

"No!" Mimorin screamed.

For some reason—no, the reason was obvious—Mimorin barged in between the two of them. She stole Haruhiro away from Tokimune and tucked him under her arm. Haruhiro wasn't an object, though.

"No kissing," Mimorin said fiercely. "This is mine."

"Since when did I belong to you?" Haruhiro muttered. "Come on, let go of me..."

"Wah ha ha!" Tokimune gave a thumbs up. "Anyway, we owe you one, Haruhiro. A big one. I'm a forgetful guy, but I don't forget this kind of stuff often."

"Not often, huh?" muttered Haruhiro. "So it's not an absolute thing."

"I rarely forget," said Tokimune.

"That's fine. Really. Whatever..."

"If you need something, come talk to me anytime," said Tokimune. "If it's for you guys, the Tokkis are ready to break a leg, two legs even, for you. I won't lend you money, but I'll lend you my life."

"Money's more valuable than your life?" Haruhiro asked skeptically.

"No. When money gets involved, it complicates things, you know? I don't like that. I'm the type that would rather give out money than lend it. So, if you need money, ask me to give it to you, and I'll give you everything I have. Not that I have any savings."

Haruhiro blinked. "You don't?"

"Yeah. None."

"Me neither," Tada said, with an attitude like, *What're you saying an obvious thing like that for, moron?*

"I've got, like, almost nothing, too, I guess?" said Kikkawa.

"I have nothing," Mimorin said clearly.

"Anna-san has money, yeah! Like, five hundred gold?! Ha ha ha! *It's joke!* I maybe have thirty silver, yeah?!"

What about Inui, who departed for the Dusk Realm? Haruhiro wondered. *None of my concern, I guess.*

While Haruhiro struggled to get away from Mimorin, his teammates—Kuzaku, Merry, Yume, and Shihoru—exchanged glances. Everyone seemed too dumbfounded to do anything.

The Tokkis. These people were worse than they had thought. With how ridiculous they all were, it was a wonder they had survived this long. What was more, they seemed to be having more fun than anyone.

Was this a viable lifestyle, too? Haruhiro really couldn't approve, but even if someone rejected the way they lived, the Tokkis probably wouldn't care. But, well, Ranta might be comparatively similar to the Tokkis.

Speaking of Ranta, he's being unusually quiet. The moment Haruhiro thought that, Ranta sprang at him.

"Haruhiroooooooooooooo!"

"Wah!" Haruhiro cried.

He didn't know what had driven Ranta mad, but Ranta was pressing the tip of Lightning Sword Dolphin up against Haruhiro's cheek. It stabbed him a bit.

"Wh-what are you doing? It's stabbing... Huh?"

"I knew I wasn't imagining it..." Ranta threw Lightning Sword Dolphin away and started crawling on the ground. He didn't seem to be apologizing to Haruhiro. He must have been depressed. "Dammit... This is awful... Seriously... Seriously... Seriously... Seriously..."

"Wh-what's up?" Haruhiro asked.

"There, there." Mimorin still wasn't letting Haruhiro go.

"Nothing's up..." Ranta punched the ground. "My Lightning Sword Dolphiiiiin! Its shocky effeeeect! It's goooone! On the way back, when I hit a cultist, I thought I noticed something weeeeird..."

"Wow." Kikkawa picked up Lightning Sword Dolphin and touched the blade. "You think it was, like, you know? It had a limited number of charges, or something?"

"This isn't what I was promiiiiised!" Ranta wailed. "I only threw away Betrayer because I got Lightning Sword Dolphin! This isn't Lightning Sword Dolphin anymoooore!"

"Y'see." Yume looked at him, as if to say, *Serves you right.* "Told you it was a waste. It's 'cause you do these wasteful things that stuff like this ends up happenin' to you, don't you think?"

"Shut up! Shut up! Just *shut up*!" Ranta screamed. "Haruhiroooo! You jerk! What're you gonna do about this?! How're you gonna make it up to meeeeeeeeeee?!"

"It's not my problem," said Haruhiro. "No matter how I look at it, this isn't my fault."

"Well, you know." Tokimune patted Ranta on the back. "Just give it up, and try to forget, okay?"

"Like I could forgeeeet! I lost Betrayer while saving you people, so, basically, it's all your fault, isn't iiiiit?!" Ranta screamed.

"Ha ha ha!" Tokimune laughed. "You could say that, huh? Well, let's go looking for another one. A good weapon. Okay?"

"Ooooooooooooh—that's not a bad idea, huh?" Ranta bellowed excitedly.

"I've had enough," Shihoru muttered to herself.

Merry was nodding. Kuzaku wasn't saying anything, but he almost certainly agreed.

"By the way," Mimorin said, finally releasing Haruhiro.

He was in a better state than when she had him under her arm, but Mimorin lifted Haruhiro up and sat him down in front of her. They were facing each other, kneeling formally, with the expressionless Mimorin looking down at Haruhiro.

"Haruhiro," she said.

"Yes?"

"Haruhiro, you're not pitiful. The way you're not pitiful, and you try so hard—that's cute."

"I see," he said.

Huh? I wonder why. I feel like I'm going to grin.

Was Haruhiro feeling... happy? Apparently, yes. Not pitiful. It wasn't much of a compliment, but maybe because it was so moderate, that actually made it easier to accept and he felt happier about it.

"You think?" he said. "Well... Thanks."

"I..."

"Yes?"

"I want to raise—"

Did she start to say, "Raise you as a pet" just now?! Haruhiro thought.

Mimorin cleared her throat, then corrected herself. "I want to go out with you. Please, go out with me."

Haruhiro quietly bowed his head to her.

I'm happy, Mimorin. No, I really am happy. Happy that you gave me that moderate bit of recognition. But this and that are two separate things.

Haruhiro wasn't strong-willed, but he could say what he had to. He could say it clearly.

"I'm sorry."

afterword

There's a game called *Romancing SaGa 2*. It was originally for the Super Famicom, so there may not be many of you who have played it (there's an iPhone port, too).

As you're aware (?), *Romancing SaGa* is an RPG series that sells itself on its open scenario. In *RS2*, you play as a succession of your original protagonist's heirs. I liked this system of succession, and I thought *Fire Emblem: Genealogy of the Holy War* was satisfying for the same reasons, but I played *RS2* years before it, so it's the one that's had the deeper impact on me.

In Japanese RPGs (or rather, console games in general), there's a scenario to follow, and you enjoy it from the perspective of a single protagonist. However, in *RS*, as I already mentioned, the scenario is open, and depending on how you advance through the story, it changes a little. *RS2* takes this a bit further with its succession across generations, and it allows the player to create the history of the game world.

I was charmed by this RPG, which had a lot in common with one of Koei's historical simulation games. (By the way, I like historical simulation games, too. Though I usually stop playing before I finish them.)

I really doubt I'll do it in *Grimgar*, but someday I'd like to write a fantasy novel where we watch history be created through a succession of the protagonist's heirs. Or rather, I want to play a game like that with modern technology. Could someone please make it? Actually, is there going to be a new *SaGa* game? In early December 2014, when I'm writing this afterword, there's still no word on one. I have hope, based on certain signs, that there will be one announced soon. (Later, *SaGa 2015* (temporary title) was announced. Yay!)

When I was in middle school, there was a period where I was reading magazines and studying programming by myself, so if things had gone completely wrong, I might have gone into game development. If that had happened, what sort of game would I have attempted to make before becoming frustrated with it and becoming a piece of human refuse? I wonder about that.

I've run out of pages.

To my editor, K, to Eiri Shirai-san, to the designers of KOME-WORKS among others, to everyone involved in production and sales of this book, and finally to all of you people now holding this book, I offer my heartfelt appreciation and all of my love. My other work, which shares the same setting as *Grimgar*—*What's Wrong with a Hero Being Jobless?*—will have its third volume published at the same time as this volume published at the same time as this volume, so I ask you to please read that one, too, if you can. Now I lay down my pen for today.

I hope we will meet again.

Ao Jyumonji